The water exploded twenty feet in front of the Sanger Alley Cat.

"The cutter's coming fast and it's got long-range bazookas," Ganja shouted.

Another explosion in the water, this time just to the port stern, nearly turned the speedboat over.

"Hang on!" Kane yelled as he pushed the Cat's jet turbines to their full 1000 horsepower and started a sharp zigzag pattern to avoid the shells.

Two more exploded on either side of the great white wake the speeding Cat created.

"We'll outrun her into the open seas!" Kane shouted, veering out direct toward the horizon. "Another ten minutes and . . ."

"Look out there," Miles yelled, pointing at two tiny specks in the sky behind them. "Choppers!"

In a matter of seconds they could see the two UH-1X Dragonflies eating up the distance between them at 250 miles an hour, their rockets and twin machine guns already spitting fire.

Getting back to Barracuda Reef was going to be a problem . . .

Other books in the **KANE'S WAR** series:

#1 KANE'S WAR
#2 THE ASSASSIN

KANE'S WAR

#3 DEATH WAVES

Nick Stone

IVY BOOKS • NEW YORK

Ivy Books
Published by Ballantine Books

Produced by Butterfield Press, Inc.
133 Fifth Avenue
New York, New York 10003

Library of Congress Catalog Card Number: 87-90783

ISBN 0-8041-0024-1

Manufactured in the United States of America

First Edition: July 1987

DEATH WAVES

Prologue

"Karen, Karen, get up!"

Karen Aztec opened her eyes and then covered them with her hand as she looked up at her friend's face. The strong Virgin Island sun was directly over Nancy's head, framing her hair and making the stray brown tendrils look as if she were wearing a fiery crown.

It took Karen a few seconds to remember that she was on the deck of the *Elgin*, a small sailboat. She had closed her eyes for a moment, feeling the caressing warmth of the sun, and must have fallen asleep. Now Nancy was shaking her shoulder, pulling her away from the delicious nap and her dream about Ben Kane. Nancy probably wanted to warn her about falling asleep without putting on suntan lotion.

"I put on lotion," Karen mumbled. "Number ten, like you told me."

"No! Come on, get up!"

There was a sense of urgency in Nancy's voice, and Karen made an effort to rise.

"What?"

Nancy pointed off the port side of the boat. Karen followed her finger and noticed a smudge on the horizon.

"It's a boat, what about it?"

Nancy handed her friend the Commander binoculars. They were a gift from Nancy's father, made by Steiner with an illuminated compass and range finder. Karen held the green armor up to her eyes and focused in on the field. She saw what was troubling her friend. The boat ap-peared to be on fire. Thick black smoke was pouring out of the vessel's pilot house.

"What should we do?" Nancy asked her.

Karen felt a twinge of annoyance. Since they had arrived on the Virgin Islands from Florida three weeks ago, Nancy had deferred every decision to her.

"What do *you* think we should do?" Karen asked her.

Her friend made a face and shrugged her plump shoulders.

Karen sighed. There was a boat on fire and perhaps some lives in danger.

"Well, the first law of the sea is to help someone in trouble. I guess we should go over there."

She moved toward the crisp white sails. Nancy nodded and scampered to the wheel.

Now they were edging closer to the smoking craft. The thick, billowing black smoke was still coming from the pilot house of the fishing boat.

Karen couldn't see any flames on the deck, but from the amount of smoke, below deck must have been an inferno.

"Nancy, radio our position. We should let the Coast Guard know what's going on."

"Do you see anybody?"

"No, and the liferaft is still on board. They must be below," Karen said. "I can't make out the name of the boat. Can you?"

The fishing vessel had a net tossed over its side, blocking out its numbers and name.

Nancy shook her head. "No, I'll radio."

They were ten miles south of Bovocoap Point. Karen used the binocs to search the water. Sometimes people panicked and forgot about the liferafts. But the sea was calm . . . and empty.

Karen maneuvered the *Elgin* to a few feet off the fishing boat's bow. It was a twenty-eight-footer, much the worse for wear, with rusted railings and patches of exposed wood with peel-ing paint.

"Hellooo," Karen called.

There was no answer.

3

"Should we try to board?" Nancy asked.

Karen didn't have a chance to answer.

Two men, wearing identical black pants and black turtlenecks, stood up from the deck where they were hiding. They were mean-looking men, dark, unshaven. In their hands, each held an ominous-looking automatic weapon.

CHAPTER 1

Ben Kane pulled off the bright red helmet and wiped the sea spray off the face plate. He turned to the barrel-shaped man next to him, who also was removing his helmet and cursing the seat restraints. Chief Bukowski hated to be strapped into anything, even if it was Ben Kane's newest playtoy.

"What was the time, Chief?" Kane asked him.

The Chief checked his stopwatch and then looked at it again. "That can't be right," he said, shaking his head. "We couldn't have been cruising along at 108 miles an hour."

"We sure as hell could have." Kane laughed and

slapped Bukowski on the back. "I told you this little cat was the fastest thing on the ocean."

The "little cat" was a Sanger Alley Cat with a Pratt Whitney PT-8 jet turbine bolted on to it. The helicopter turbine could generate over a thou-sand horsepower on takeoff and power the boat to a high of 116 mph.

"You know, Ben, if Gordon hears about this rig, he's going to start to believe all those stories about you smuggling drugs into the Keys."

Kane nodded. Walt Gordon was a tough retired police captain from New York City who had fallen in love with the Virgin Islands and ac-cepted a job as U.S. Marshall for the American islands. As Kane's charter outfit, Caribbean Dream, grew larger each year, the local authori-ties kept a close eye on its activities.

"Let 'em talk, Chief," Kane said. "We've got more important things to do. What do you think it will take to get this baby up to a hundred and fifty?"

"A miracle."

"John Ross Cobb hit two hundred and six."

"Sure, and then he and his boat disintegrated."

Kane thought about that. "That's because the salt water crystallized on his turbine blades. We suck the air in from grills around the engine for cooling, but the intake air comes from under the back seat, which acts as a splash guard."

"You'll need a bigger boat to handle a power package large enough to hit one-fifty."

"Maybe not. There's a six-hundred-horsepower package that weighs less than a hundred and fifty pounds. I've heard about fifty-seven-foot catamarans with twin 2600-horsepower jet engines."

"I'm telling you now, Ben, you won't get me on that one. Call Ganja if you need a first mate."

As if on cue, the Si-Tex Compact 55 crackled, and Ganja's voice came on. Ben picked up the small hand mike and responded.

"Ben, remember before you left the Reef this morning we heard that report about the yacht they found floating off St. John?"

"The one owned by the German beer baron?"

"Right. Well, there's been a report of another yacht missing in the same area. *Kudos*, the Greek dude's ship."

"Isn't that the area Karen and Nancy went sailing in?" Ben said, his level of concern rising.

"Near to it, Skip."

"Give them a call and get back to me. Over."

Ganja Grant was back on Barracuda Reef, the nerve center for Caribbean Dream. The idyllic harbor, developed by Ben's friend, Mike Mulhaney, housed a dockyard where Ben repaired his fleet, and the Rainbow Keg Inn, where Ben and his cohorts went for repairs. Both successful spots were owned and operated by the legendary Mike Mulhaney and his lovely spitfire of a daughter, Michelle Mulhaney.

Ben lived aboard the fifty-foot teak-decked *Wu Li*, a splendidly appointed Chinese junk harbored at Barracuda Reef. His offices were not far away, in an ultra-modern two-story building that housed some of the most sophisticated communi-cations gear in the Caribbean.

Ganja kept tabs on all of the sixty-eight-boat armada that made up Caribbean Dream, as well as monitoring the airwaves for weather and navigational problems.

Like Chief Bukowski, Ganja Grant had served with Ben Kane in the "brown water" Navy that had fought in Vietnam. When the war finally came to a close, people like the Chief and Lieutenant Commander Kane found themselves cut loose as "experts in a specialty no longer needed by the Navy" and discharged.

Kane had drifted, landing in the U.S. Virgins on a brief stopover before he headed up to the States. But somehow he never seemed to set a date to leave, and had stayed to make his home in the magnificent tropical paradise.

Hiring out as skipper for bigger fishing boats, Kane had eventually put enough away to get his first deep-sea vessel, and the Caribbean Dream charter service was born. As his reputation grew, so did his fleet, and eventually he'd become the owner of the largest private fleet in the Virgins. Some said that his fleet grew too fast, too soon to be financed by hard work and legal loans alone, but nobody could prove the rumors.

Soon, Kane needed a permanent crew he could trust. He rounded up his old buddies from The

Nam, who were floating around like so much flotsam, and hired them in important positions at the Caribbean Dream.

Chief Bukowski, whose real first name was Walter but whom everyone called Chief, was one of the three key members of his staff. Bukowski had been a Master Petty Officer under Kane, and the preeminent "fixer" in the southeast Asian theater. If Kane needed it and the Navy couldn't provide it, Bukowski got it. Bukowski loved riverine duty—it got him out from most of the regular Navy regulations. The only thing the Chief couldn't fix was his age. When he hit thirty years' service, the Navy mustered him out. He'd leaped at the chance to get back into small boats under Kane's command.

Somehow or other, the Chief continued appropriating material and services for Kane when other charter outfits tied them up. The five-foot ten-inch, two-hundred-twenty-pound, perpetu-ally sunburned Bukowski could bribe the local desk sergeant into letting some drunken crew members be released, or calm down the locals who wanted to lynch an offensive charter cus-tomer.

Billy "Ganja" Grant was a street-smart black man from Harlem who had served as a gunner under Kane in the Mekong. He adapted to the Virgin Island lifestyle by sporting Rasta dreadlocks and speaking a patois developed from dialects of half the islands in the Caribbean. He never touched alcohol, but loved his smoke, or

9

"ganja." He lived in a ramshackle hut near the Reef, spending money as freely as he made it, but always making sure to send some of it back home to his brothers and sisters on St. Nicholas Avenue. The natives trusted the "ganja man," and he had been a terrific help to Ben Kane by passing on local inside information, in addition to his expert radio skills.

The third member of Kane's Caribbean staff was the enigmatic Miles. Tall, thin, completely unpredictable, there was no one in the world he trusted completely but Ben Kane. Miles was a SEAL who'd seen his whole outfit wiped out in a forty-second firefight. He survived by standing nostril deep in the swampy Mekong for thirty-six hours. It was Ben Kane who had come back and risked his own life to save Miles.

Expert in weapons and deep-sea rescue, Miles was invaluable to the hundreds of Caribbean Dream clients stranded on little atolls or broken-down boats throughout the season.

The radio crackled with Ganja's voice. "Done. They called in about a boat on fire. Said they were going to help. I checked back, and the radio's dead."

"Got the coordinates?" Ben asked him.

He read off the longitude and latitude and Ben waited as Chief Bukowski found the spot on the charts.

"We can be there in about fifteen minutes if we full-throttle this buggy," Bukowski told him.

"Ganja, we're going to take a look-see. Keep the channel open."

"Okay, Skip. Out," Ganja said.

CHAPTER 2

The women were too frightened to speak and stood shaking on the deck of the *Elgin*. The two men aimed their guns at their breasts.

"You have radio on board. You called someone and gave position, yes?" the one called Mahmout barked.

Nancy looked at Karen.

"No, there was no time. We saw the fire and we sailed to help you," she lied.

Mahmout walked over to Nancy and stood in front of her menacingly.

"Is true?" he said sharply.

She cowered, but managed to nod her head.

"Good!"

"What happened to the fire?" Karen asked, gathering her courage.

Mahmout looked at his partner Sidi, and they both laughed. "This is fire." He held up a small steel canister. It was an Army-issue smoke bomb.

"We spin our web like spider and wait for unsuspecting fly to get stuck," Sidi said.

"Look, I have some money in my bag, and my ring and watch are worth something. Just take it and leave us alone."

"We're no thief," Sidi said.

Karen swallowed hard. "I don't understand."

"You take a ride with us and find out," Mahmout said.

Nancy and Karen were dragged over to the fishing boat and down into the hold. There was a freezerlike compartment where the fish were held after a catch. The freezer hadn't been turned on and the stench from dead fish made the women gag.

"Please don't lock us in here," Nancy pleaded, but the door closed behind them and they heard it being locked.

It was pitch dark. The smell was overwhelming.

"Oh, God," Nancy wailed and began to cry.

Holding her nose, Karen felt around the edges of the door. She moved around the cramped compartment looking for some way out. There wasn't any.

"What are we going to do, Karen?"

"I don't know."

"They're going to kill us," Nancy said fearfully.

"If they wanted to, they could have killed us when they came aboard."

"First they're going to rape and torture us."

"Shut up, Nancy! Shut up and let me think."

The boat lurched forward. By the loud noises of the men on deck, it was time for celebrating. Nancy heard them over the din of the engines.

Wherever they were going was probably nearby, Karen reasoned. That was why Mahmout had been so concerned if they had radioed their position. Ben Kane had told her this area wasn't well traveled and to watch out for a strong current from some uncharted islands in the vicinity. She hoped the charter service knew enough to follow up their radio call. It was their only chance.

There was no one aboard the *Elgin*. Chief searched the deck, and Ben went down to check the galley. When he came back up, his jaw was set in a tight line.

"Anything, Chief?"

Bukowski shook his head. "There's a towel on deck, suntan lotion, open can of soda—but no sign of the ladies."

"They had a pot of coffee brewed on the stove. It was still warm," Ben said thoughtfully. "And all their valuables are in their purses." He stared out over the water. "Tell Ganja where to pick up the *Elgin*. I just had an idea."

Bukowski nodded. He radioed the *Elgin*'s position and joined Ben back on the Cat.

"What're you thinking, Ben?" Chief asked him.

"All three of the boats that had trouble had one thing in common. The women were missing."

"I don't follow," Bukowski said.

"The German fellow was found shot, and Kalaxis and his crew were all killed and left floating. But none of the women were found."

Bukowski thought it over.

"Slavers! We haven't had white slavers around here for five or six years."

"Well, they're back," Kane said. "And I've got an idea where they are."

"Let's hear it."

"A small fishing boat's been seen in these waters for the past few days now. Twin engine, low draw, with just enough cabin for a cold storage bin. If that's the slavers' boat, they'd need a land base in the area to work from while they look for more victims."

Bukowski nodded. "Good thinking, except that there's no safe harbor around here."

"What about Pelican Cove?" Kane asked, pointing to the small atoll on the charts.

"Pelican! You can't get a boat in there. Water's too shallow."

"Not for that small a fishing boat it's not!"

Before Chief could reply, Kane had started the

engines. He turned the boat north toward Pelican Cove, leaving a huge wake behind them.

Kane's hunch paid off.

As they cut the engines and glided to the south end of the small island, they spied the fishing boat anchored on the far side of the tiny natural harbor.

"Nobody on the beach," Chief observed through the binoculars. "We still got enough speed for me to pull her close enough for us to—"

"Hold her steady, Chief. No sense us both risking our necks," Kane interrupted. "I'll swim ashore and see if I can surprise them. You sit tight and wait for my signal. If there's no sign in three hours, call Miles and get reinforcements."

The Chief looked skeptical. "Alone, without a gun? What are you gonna do, kill the bastards with kindness?"

"Something like that," Kane said, smiling as he shrugged on his wet suit. "Remember, three hours."

Chief nodded, then watched Kane slip over the side and make for the island.

CHAPTER 3

As Kane approached shore, he looked around for cover. Spotting a large bougainvillea a few feet off the beach, he darted toward it. As he ran, he detected something moving in a clearing to his left. It was a man walking slowly in the opposite direction. Kane kept the man in view as he ran into the underbrush, and then followed him into the island's junglelike vegetation.

The man came to a shack that was well hidden by the large flame trees. Ben noted that there were leaves on the small structure's roof. That would stop anything in the air from spotting the wooden hut. Interesting.

Kane waited five minutes and then moved closer. The front of the hut had a simple wooden door. There were two windows on either side. Ben carefully made his way to the back, thinking that there might be another window.

What he saw stopped him in his tracks. He had seen cages like that before. The small bamboo pens, called *takara* by the Viet Cong, that usually held American GIs.

Kane had been part of an assault landing to liberate a village along the Mekong. After the vicious firefight and Charlie's retreat into the jungle, they had found six soldiers in the small bamboo cages. The men had been beaten and starved, their open sores a banquet table for the mosquitoes and vermin. The feelings of shock and disgust came back full force as he saw five women penned up like animals.

Three of the women were stripped naked. Nancy and Karen were wearing bathing suits. From his vantage point, Kane could see that Nancy and Karen seemed to be unharmed. He couldn't tell how the other three were. They were lying down, apparently sleeping.

Keeping one eye on the hut, he made his way to the cages. He was practically next to them when Nancy spun around and saw him.

"Ben!" she gasped.

Kane put his finger to his lips to signal her to keep quiet. Karen whirled and saw him. A big smile crossed her lips.

Ben didn't waste any time. He looked over the steel padlock and grunted. The doors of the small pens were sealed up tight. He couldn't bust them out of there without a key.

"Are you okay?" he asked in a whisper.

"Yes," Karen told him. "We've only been here a short while. The other three have been here for days. Something is wrong with the little German girl over there." She gestured toward the second cage. "Coco says she's in shock."

"Who's Coco?" Ben wanted to know.

"I'm Coco," the redhead next to Nancy said. "My name is Colette but they all call me Coco. I hope you're not the whole rescue party."

"You're stuck with little old me," Ben told her.

Coco shook her head. "Terrific."

"I've got to get the keys to break you out of here. Why don't you call a guard out, Coco. I'll take care of the rest."

"But you don't even have a gun on you," she said.

"I like to travel light," Ben told her. He stepped behind a nearby tree.

Coco waited for him to take his cover, then started yelling for a guard.

The door of the hut opened and a head stuck out.

"Pipe down. Just keep your mouth shut, if you know what's good for you."

"Come here, Andre," Coco said. "Just come here for a second. I've got to talk to you," she purred.

"You hold it until later like everybody else."

Ben noticed the man's thick French accent.

"No, that's not it. Just come here for a second. I won't bite you."

"Sacre bleu," Andre mumbled under his breath, but he stepped out of the hut and walked toward the cages.

Kane waited for him to get close, then pounced like a big cat. His arms snaked around Andre's throat to cut off his windpipe. The Frenchman tried to yell, but no sounds could come out with Kane cutting off his air supply. Andre tried to break free, but Ben held him in a viselike grip. His eyes bugged, his face turned beet red, his legs flailed out of control, and then he stopped moving. Kane let him drop unconscious to the ground. Another ten seconds in the Korean choke lock and the man would have been dead.

"Impressive!" Coco said.

Ben searched Andre's pockets and came up with a set of steel keys.

"That's it!" Coco told him. "They all carry their own set."

Ben stood up and tried one of the keys in the first cage, where the young German girl was now standing and encouraging him in her native tongue.

The first key didn't fit. Kane tried the next one and the lock clicked. He swung the bamboo door open and she stepped out. He motioned with his hand for the girl to wait next to him.

He opened the lock. The girl didn't move.

"Greta! Greta!" the other girl whispered, trying to get her out of her stupor.

Ben touched her arm gently. It was the wrong thing to do. The girl began screaming at the top of her lungs. The girl was beyond reason. The murder of her parents, the imprisonment, the rough treatment by her captors had driven her past the breaking point.

Kane could see there was no way to stop the girl from screaming and bringing out one of the other captors. To make matters worse, Andre was starting to stir on the ground.

The door of the hut opened and two men came out. One was tall and looked like an American. The other was dark, with Semitic features. They both carried automatic weapons, which they leveled at Kane. Ben pushed the German girl out of the line of fire and dived for the thick brush. He heard the hum of bullets pass his ear as he rolled into the dense grass and disappeared be-hind the tall trees that surrounded the clearing. He knew he was safe for the moment. You could lose a herd of elephants in the lush Caribbean vegetation. Practically invisible, he stopped and watched only forty feet away from the girls in their cages.

The two men were joined by another Semitic man, who dashed into the forest looking for Ben. He headed in the wrong direction.

Ben saw the one who looked like an American

push the German girl back into her bamboo cell. He locked her up again and helped Andre to his feet. The Frenchman rubbed his neck where Kane had applied the choke hold.

"Who was he?" the tall man shouted at Greta. "What the hell was he doing here?"

The German girl continued to scream at the top of her lungs.

The man reached into the cage and slapped her hard across the face. "Shuttup!" he bellowed.

Greta continued, her eyes glassy, her face contorted.

The other German girl, evidently her sister, began to speak to her in a soft, soothing tone. In a few seconds, Greta stopped yelling.

"That's better," the American grunted.

"He jumped me from behind, Jake," Andre said, turning toward Coco. "This one. It was she who yelled for me to come out."

"Oh, she did, did she?" Jake eyed the redhead. She looked back at him defiantly. "Who's your new friend, Coco?"

"Screw you, Jake."

The man who'd gone to look for Kane came back into the clearing.

"He's gone," he said, cursing.

"No way, Sidi. I think our Mister-Do-Gooder is watching us and listening to us right now," Jake said, looking around.

Reaching into the waistband of his pants, Jake pulled out a snub-nosed 7.65mm Mauser. He pointed it at Coco's head. "If he don't come out by the time I count three, the redhead's a corpse."

Sidi conversed with the other man in rapid-fire Arabic.

"Shoot this one," Sidi said in English, pointing to Nancy. "The redhead will fetch a better price."

Jake grunted, but reluctantly shifted his aim.

"One. Two."

Nancy stared in horror.

Kane walked out of the forest. "Put your gun down," he told Jake.

Jake turned the gun on Kane. "Well now, if it ain't Mr. Cousteau."

Concentrating on the gun, Kane moved closer, unaware that Andre had slipped behind him until he felt a hard punch in the center of his back that sent him flying to the ground. Andre kicked him hard in the belly, then aimed another kick at Ben's head. Ben was able to move just slightly, so the kick turned out to be a glancing shot rather than a knockout blow.

"Don't kill him," Jake said, pulling Andre away. "At least not until we find out if he's got anyone with him."

Andre reached down and turned Ben's head. Kane pretended to be unconscious.

"He's not dead," Andre told the others. "What do we do with him?"

"Aw, the hell with him," Jake said. "He looks like a hard case. He won't give us no information. Put a bullet in him and good riddance."

"No, not here," one of the Arabs said. "We use this island again. No good if authorities find body here. No time to bury him."

"So what's your idea, Mahmout?"

"Carry him to chopper, then kill, and drop in ocean."

"Like hell I will. If he can't walk, he buys it now," Jake said, kneeling down next to Kane. "Come on, Sleeping Beauty. Your nap is over."

Ben moaned and then slowly raised his head. The ground started to spin crazily, and a feeling of nausea coursed through him. He fought a soothing cool black mist calling to him, knowing that if he passed out, he was dead. Slowly, he made it to his feet.

"You made my friend Andre a little angry."

"Shh, listen!" Mahmout said, holding his hand in the air like a traffic cop.

Ben heard it, too. It was the sound of a chopper, a big one.

"All right. Get the girls out of the cages and onto the beach," Jake commanded. "Move!"

The Arabs were already unlocking the girls and herding them together. The two German sisters clutched each other tightly. The younger one moved as if in a trance.

"Let's go!" Andre yelled. "To the beach, now!"

Kane was pushed along behind them, Jake's Mauser poking a hole in his back.

CHAPTER 4

It had only been an hour, and Kane knew that Chief Bukowski wouldn't make a move until three hours had gone by. Even then, it would take at least another hour before Ganja could lead a group of men to Pelican.

The chopper flew in low over the water and hovered a foot or two over the sandy beach. It settled down in a cloud like a big insect.

Kane guessed this chopper could hold twelve people. He already knew that he wasn't going to make the full trip. He guessed there would be two men on board. He was right.

They were a ragtag duo, the kind of scum you see in a waterfront bar. After the copter landed, they shook hands with Jake and the Arabs and made all kinds of obscene remarks and gestures toward the girls. Ben noted, however, that they were very careful not to put their hands on the women. They must have been scared plenty to follow orders not to touch.

They asked about Kane, and Jake told them.

"Hey, see what happens when you try to be a hero," one of them said. "Bet you thought you'd free the princesses and get to bang them all yourself." He laughed.

"When do we get them on board?" Andre asked impatiently.

"Right now!" Jake said.

He pushed Kane behind the women and herded them to the door of the waiting chopper.

Suddenly, there was a sound in the air like a giant swarm of bees. Kane turned and spotted the three Hughes 1550 helicopters coming in low over the treetops.

Before anyone else could react, Kane pushed the girls down on the ground. It was a good thing he did. The lead chopper raked the area with machine-gun bullets, cutting down one of the kidnappers who had landed only moments before.

"Take cover over there," Jake yelled to Andre, pointing toward a sand dune.

They dodged bullets and made it behind the dune.

"Who is it, Ben? The Coast Guard?" Karen asked him.

One of the choppers landed. The two Arabs were down on their knees blasting at it with their automatic weapons. Another chopper hovered over the large white Grumman, making sure it couldn't escape. The third copter circled around to the dune, its turrets laying down a shower of lead.

The three Hughes craft were camouflage green with the word SECURITY painted on the underbelly next to a logo that looked like the letter M on top of a rock.

"They're not the Coast Guard," Ben said, watching as the door of the chopper opened and three green-and-red-uniform-clad soldiers leaped out.

Mahmout and Sidi cut down the first two, but the third soldier tossed an M34 grenade, scatter-ing a charge of white phosphorus at the two Arabs. They were torched into writhing, scream-ing fireballs. The smell of burning flesh filled the heavy mid-afternoon air.

"Oh, God,"Karen said, watching the carnage.

"They're another group of kidnappers," Nancy wailed. "We'll never get away."

"Put your guns down and surrender!" a voice ordered over a loudspeaker in the chopper that hovered over the Grumman.

Two of the men tried to make a run for the forest. A sharpshooter using an M16 pumped a

29

slug into each one of them. The man knew what he was doing; the bullets exploded their skulls like ripe watermelons.

That left Jake and Andre.

The two Hughes choppers were now on the ground. The one hovering over the Grumman was probably the command vehicle, talking to the men via walkie-talkie and directing their actions.

It wasn't going to be easy flushing the two slavers out from the dune. Ben saw they were carrying Ingram M10 SMGs. He knew they had plenty of clips in their pockets and on their belts.

"You have one more chance to surrender!" the loudspeaker boomed again.

The slavers put up a volley of bullets in response.

The two choppers on the ground had emptied of soldiers. Kane counted eighteen in all, with the two dead on the ground. Kane watched as the men moved with absolute military precision, each one standing ten feet from the other, forming a semicircle around the sand dune. They moved as one, switching the M16s from single shot to automatic.

"I will count to three," the man in the lead chopper said, his voice echoing slightly on the speaker.

"One . . ."

There was no sound from the dune. The surf in the background whooshed on the white sand of the shore.

"Two . . ."

Ben thought he saw Andre stand. If he did, it was only for a split second and then he was down again.

"Three."

Now the men began to move forward, the semicircle closing on the dune. The muzzles of the sixteen guns coughed a steady stream of bullets into the sputtering sand.

Something strange was happening, but Ben couldn't quite figure it out. Jake and Andre had their weapons going also. Some of the soldiers fell in the initial bursts. Still, the soldiers marched forward, seeming to be oblivious to the danger in front of them.

That in itself didn't surprise Kane. He had seen fighters march into sure death, making a human bridge in a swamp so their comrades could get to the enemy by walking over their corpses. The Chinese and Iranians waged war by sending human waves into battle. There was something else that was making this scene odd.

Then Kane realized what was unusual. As the semicircle tightened like a noose in a ring of death, the uniformed men walked forward in complete silence. Kane had never seen anything like this. When men fought together, they usually psyched themselves with a lot of yelling and cursing. Kane had even heard men roar like animals. Yet these men walked forward into gunfire without a sound and watched their comrades fall around them—all the while maintaining absolute silence.

31

A wild thought struck Kane for a second—that these green-uniformed men might in actuality be some kind of state-of-the-art robots. Then Kane looked at the two that had been shot down by the Arabs. The torn skin and bone and spilled blood were all too real.

There were two other alternatives: incredible training and dedication . . . or drugs.

They moved in closer and closer, with no regard for their own safety.

Jake and Andre stood up to run and were literally cut in half. Karen had to turn her head away.

When the shooting finally stopped, Kane counted seven of the soldiers left alive. They turned, responding to some unheard command, and double-timed it back to the first of the three choppers that had landed.

"You people near the white chopper, please stay where you are," the loudspeaker voice ordered.

Kane and the women stood up and waited for the third green Hughes to settle to the ground a few yards away.

The first man to emerge was a lean six-footer wearing jeans and a green T-shirt. Another man followed, carrying what turned out to be green jumpsuits with the same insignia as on the copters embroidered over the breast pockets.

"Is everybody all right?" the first man asked.

Kane recognized it as the voice on the speaker system. He shook hands with Kane as the man who followed him off the chopper handed jumpsuits to each of the women.

The redhead held up her suit.

"Not bad," Coco said, putting hers on.

The German girl, still in shock, was helped by her sister.

"I'm Lincoln Mica. Everybody calls me Link. Does anybody need a doctor? I can have one here in about twenty minutes or so."

"The little German girl seems to be in shock," Karen told him, walking over and brushing the girl's hair off of her face.

"Should we get a doctor for you?" Link asked her.

"She doesn't speak English," Nancy told him. "Oh," Mica said. He started speaking German to the girl. She didn't respond, but her sister spoke for her. Mica nodded his head.

"Are you German, Mr. Mica?" Coco wanted to know.

"No, but I seem to be able to learn languages fairly easily," Mica said, shrugging. "The girl will be taken to a hospital on St. John's. Her sister will stay with her."

Karen suddenly looked up with a start. "You said Mica?"

"That's right."

"You're Link Mica . . . of Mica Industries?"

Link smiled. He had a disarming full-bodied smile with just a touch of "aw shucks" innocence. His deep-set brown eyes and thick, windblown hair reminded Ben of a young Gary Cooper.

"Guilty," he replied.

"I'm Karen Aztec."

Mica put both of his hands on the top of his head. "I don't believe it! Now I am glad we got here before those creeps took off."

"Do you two know each other?" Kane asked, slightly bewildered.

"Ben, this is my new boss. He's the man Doctor Townsend and I will be working for."

Link made a wincing face. "Can't we say working *with*. We're all on the team—me included."

"How in the world did you find us?" Karen asked him.

"And where did you get your security force?" Kane wanted to know. "I've never seen a group of more dedicated soldiers."

Mica nodded. "They're the best in the world. Look, why don't you all join me for dinner aboard my yacht. I'm moored ten miles northeast of Mica Island. I'd be very pleased to have you, and perhaps then I could answer all of your questions. In the meantime, my helicopter will take you back to wherever you're staying."

"That's very kind of you," Karen said.

"I think I would enjoy that," Kane told him.

"Tonight at eight, then. I'll get you the chart location." Link Mica gave a wave and walked back to his chopper.

"I think I'm in love," Coco said, watching him climb aboard the craft.

"He's certainly impressive," Karen agreed.

And cold-blooded, Kane thought. Link Mica hadn't shown the slightest sign of remorse that he had lost more than half his men.

CHAPTER 5

"Where's Nancy?" Kane asked as Karen stepped aboard the *Wu Li*.

Karen looked lovely, wearing a long white dress with a crossed sash of the silky material barely covering her breasts.

"Don't get me started on her, Ben," she said huffily.

Kane smiled. "Touched a nerve, eh?"

"Do you know what kind of nerve she has? She blamed me for the fact that we were boarded by slavers and captured. She told me that it was my fault that we went to help them, and that I was to blame for ruining her entire vacation."

"Not very fair," Ben said, shaking his head in sympathy.

"Damn right it isn't fair! All I said was that the first law of the sea was to help someone in trouble. Am I right?"

"Absolutely," Ben said, taking her arm and guiding her down to the *Wu Li*'s luxurious main salon and dining area.

The fifty-foot teak-decked Chinese junk was well appointed, with an entertainment room and bar designed to Kane's exacting specifications. He stood at the bar and poured Karen a Kahlua on the rocks, and took a chilled Absolut vodka for himself.

"So I take it she won't be chaperoning us tonight?"

"She's gone, Ben. She went back to the hotel room, packed her things, and headed for the airport."

"That's a shame," Ben said.

Karen looked at him and tried to decide if he was mocking her. She knew that Nancy and Ben didn't care for each other.

"Sarcasm I can get from my patients, Ben."

"Why shouldn't I be pleased that we'll get to spend some time alone with each other?" Ben asked her with a boyish smile.

He's very handsome, Karen thought.

He was wearing a white dinner jacket over black mohair slacks, with a tailored white silk shirt and black bowtie. His hair must have been a darker brown at one time, but the exposure to the sea air had lightened it considerably. What she really loved about his strong, masculine face were those incredible aquamarine eyes of his. She could get lost in those eyes.

"I'm afraid our time together is running out quickly," she said.

"It doesn't have to," he told her seriously.

They talked about Karen's contract with Mica Industries. Karen had agreed to live on Mica Island for three months. During that time she was to stay on the island and not have any contact with the outside world.

Ben wasn't very happy with those provisions, but Karen explained that Dr. Townsend had insisted upon them.

Dr. Robert Townsend had become a sort of demi-god for Karen. As a psychology undergraduate, she had taken a course with Townsend and had been mesmerized by the elderly man's wisdom and sensitivity. Karen felt that Dr. Townsend's influence was the most important factor in her becoming a psychologist.

Over the years, Karen and Dr. Townsend corresponded with each other and shared in each other's success. The crown jewel of the distinguished doctor's career occurred when he received a Nobel Prize for his work on behavioral modification.

Ben was convinced, after listening to Karen, that anything her mentor suggested would be all right with her—which made him glad that the good doctor was approaching eighty.

Townsend had told Karen that he would explain the need for the three-month commitment when he saw her. Karen was due to begin her job on the island in two days.

Ben looked at his ISP Aquastar watch. "There's no rush," he said, moving closer to her.

She turned to him, and they kissed. It was a long, passionate kiss that left her breathless.

"You look so beautiful," Ben told her.

He stood up and led her into the master stateroom. In moments, they were undressed and in each other's arms.

Slowly, Ben began to run a line of kisses down her jaw and to her neck and throat. He moved down the length of her collarbone and started the slight incline of her left breast. Karen felt her breathing become shallower.

His tongue darted to the hollow of her chest and then he seized her nipple between his lips. Karen found herself emitting little moans of pleasure as his lips sucked on the protruding nub of tactile flesh. He pulled back for a moment, looking at the dampness of the dark circle around her nipple. He smiled at her, and she smiled back.

After a brief moment, she grew impatient and gently put her hand around his neck to push his head down to her straining breasts. She hadn't realized that she was undulating under him. Her body was on fire and she needed him desperately.

She reached between them and found his hard shaft, so warm to her touch.

"Ben," she breathed.

His hand moved between her legs and found the silky moss surrounding her sex. He cupped her roughly, squeezing her nether lips together and making Karen gasp. One finger found her dewy crevice and he felt the warm slippery passage tightening, aching for him.

She sighed with relief when he entered her. He moved with her, in long, hard strokes of passion. He felt her clutching at him, writhing, calling his name over and over. The heat in him rose with hers. They cascaded together into a shuddering orgasm.

"Ben," Karen said in a shaky voice.

"Ummm?"

"I'm glad Nancy left."

She snuggled close to him and let herself relax in his warmth.

After a few moments, Ben sat up slowly. "If we want to get to Link's yacht, you're going to have to get dressed," he told her.

She stretched luxuriously, then whispered, "I suppose I shouldn't keep my new boss waiting."

CHAPTER 6

Ben Kane had been around boats most of his life, but Mica's yacht was the biggest pleasure boat he had ever seen in the water.

After mooring their cruiser to the yacht, Ben and Karen boarded and were greeted by a smiling, green-uniformed staff member named Roberta, who offered to give them a tour of the boat. The yacht was well over two hundred feet long, and had been designed and built to be a warship by the government of Spain. Its sleek aerodynamic design was intended to make it one of the fastest vessels of its size afloat. Mica had bought the cruiser and lavished millions on it to make it a floating palace.

The Loyalty could accommodate twenty guests, in thirteen fully air conditioned and magnificently appointed cabins. Each cabin was decorated in a different motif; the master cabin looked as if it came right out of Versailles. In each room there was a projection TV, VCR, and stereo center. One of the salons featured an extensive library of video cassettes. Kane walked through the magnificent oak bar. It was patterned after Harry's of London, filled with soft leather and brass. There was a beauty parlor/barber shop complete with a professional staff. The guide explained that the shops were strictly a convenience for the guests, since Link had a valet who took care of his own personal grooming.

Link seemed to be a water sports enthusiast. There was an impressive stock of windsurfers, four Kawasaki 350's for jet skiing, wet bikes, two heated swimming pools, state-of-the-art scuba gear, underwater photography equipment plus darkroom facilities, a 6000-psi dive compressor with a six-bottle cascade system, and full line of deep-sea fishing equipment.

There were also two Hughes helicopters on board, smaller ones than Kane had seen that afternoon, all carrying the Mica Industries insignia on their bellies.

"Would you like to see the bridge?" their hostess asked.

Ben nodded.

Link's yacht had the latest in microcomputer technology. Integrated systems allowed complete interfacing between all the modular instrumentation on board. There was a glow in the spacious cabin from the compact liquid crystal displays and analog sensors. A navigator could have all the information he needed at his fingertips, whether he was at the nav station or the helm.

Kane was very impressed with a system, manufactured by Mica Industries, that delivered 62 channels of information, including tide set and drift, target-boat speed, optimum wind angle, nautical time, speed and distance averaging, magnetic headings, water temperature and depth, and anchor alarms. The information could be fed to an autopilot, making the huge yacht fully capable of running itself without a crew.

"Just how big is *The Loyalty*?" Kane asked.

"She displaces fifteen thousand tons," their guide answered.

Kane whistled softly.

As they walked along the sparkling white deck, Kane looked straight up at what seemed to be a transmitter. It extended at least sixty feet in the air. There was a dish at the very top, a type that Kane had never seen before.

"Is Link trying to make contact with the moon?" Ben asked.

The woman laughed. "No, that's our transmitter and receiver. It's a new design, developed by Link himself. It enables him to maintain complete contact with the communication centers of the seventy-nine Mica subsidiaries located in forty-seven countries throughout the world. The Communication Room is off limits to visitors, I'm afraid. Link is concerned about industrial espionage. We have to be very cautious about that."

"Too bad," Ben said. "I would like to see it."

Roberta shrugged. "Well, I think you might want to begin dinner now. If you have time, you must see the galley, and the gym. We also have a jacuzzi and a sauna—"

"Hi!"

They turned, to see a smiling Link Mica.

"So glad you could make it," he said. "Coco is in the dining room waiting for us. Oh, isn't Nancy coming?"

"Too much excitement, I'm afraid, Mr. Mica. She took a plane back to the States," Karen told him.

"Please call me Link. And I'm terribly disappointed."

He seemed genuinely upset that Nancy wasn't going to join them. Kane tried to reconcile this concern over a stranger with the earlier absolute disregard of the deaths of his own staff of soldiers.

"I'm afraid not. I tried everything," Karen told him.

"Well, at least you two are here, and Coco, and I do have a surprise guest," he said, with a mischievous grin. "Come along and follow me. Thanks

46

for giving our guests the tour, Roberta."

"No problem, Link."

She beamed at her boss. If Link wasn't sleeping with Roberta, it wasn't because she was reluctant, Ben thought.

They followed Link past the boat deck lounge, aft deck lounge, sundeck, study, radio room, and laundry. Two fully armed guards, frozen faced and grim, stood in front of a door marked in bold red letters WARNING! KEEP OUT! That was the room Roberta had mentioned before. Link passed the spot without a word.

"Here we are," Link said.

The room was paneled in a rich mahogany. There were filigreed mirrors on one of the walls, making the room seem even larger. Over the dining table a beautiful crystal chandelier, suspended by gold chains, illuminated a massive centerpiece of fresh-cut flowers. Behind the chair that Kane presumed to be Link's was a six-by-ten bay window looking out over the ocean.

It was the kind of room that yachting magazines loved to feature in their pages, except that people like Link Mica weren't usually interested in showing the general public their possessions.

Mica motioned for them to sit, and pushed Karen's chair in under her. Coco was smiling at them, and she and Karen kissed each other on the cheek, the two becoming fast friends through adversity.

"I'm happy to tell you that Greta, the little

German girl, is doing fine. I spoke to her sister an hour ago and she told me that her aunt and uncle are flying down from Berlin to take care of them," Mica reported.

"That's wonderful," Karen said.

There was a knock on the door.

"That must be the surprise guest I was telling you about. Come in," said Mica.

The door opened revealing a silver-haired, very tan man with pleasant features. His face was lined with wrinkles, but his trim solid bearing and lively smile made him look younger than his years.

"I think you know Dr. Townsend, Karen."

"Robert!" Karen squealed, rushing to her feet and racing to give the older man a big hug.

"Karen, Karen," he said, shaking his head. "Move back a moment so I can have a look at you. Good Lord! You're absolutely smashing."

"Why, thank you."

"Oops," Townsend said, smiling. "I'm told it won't do for a man to compliment a woman on her looks these days. They call it chauvinistic, I think."

"Never you mind," Karen told him. "I think it's just fine."

"I'm afraid that women today don't know what the hell they want. It confuses the hell out of men," Coco said.

"Dr. Townsend, I'd like you to meet Coco. Coco was a good friend of Mr. Kalaxis."

Townsend's face grew serious. "I'm so sorry to

hear of his death. He was a good man, and he will be missed."

"Thank you."

"And this is Ben Kane, owner of the Caribbean Dream, one of the largest charter outfits in the Caribbean."

Mica had obviously done his homework.

Ben shook Townsend's hand and was surprised that his grip seemed so weak. It was possible that, in spite of his robust good looks, Townsend wasn't well.

"Please permit me to say something here publicly, Bob," Mica said, standing and placing his hand on Townsend's shoulder. "When I decided to develop Mica Island as a facility for Mica Industries, my first idea was to establish the place as a sort of retreat for the executives in my company all over the world. It's absolutely one of the most beautiful spots on God's great earth, and I felt very fortunate to be able to purchase it and turn it into a retreat and rehabilitation center for the Mica 'family.' Then I read Dr. Townsend's incredible work, *Addiction and Human Misery*. This was around the time that some famous movie stars were going off to the Betty Ford Clinic to take care of their alcohol addiction, and I said to myself, 'Lord, what a waste of talent.' I had been so moved by the haunting pages of Robert's book that I understood the misery that those poor souls and others like them addicted to gambling, drugs, or deviant behavior, were going through. Suddenly it dawned on me that Mica Island could be used as a facility to help such talented people. We could take the great minds, the great talents of our time, and salvage them for the good of humanity.

"With that in mind, I got in touch with the great Dr. Townsend, and asked him to head up a team to make Mica Island *the* facility for the addicted. In a few short months, I think he's changed the course of history with his miraculous cures through behavior modification."

"Link, you're much too kind," Townsend said bashfully.

"All right, I won't embarrass you anymore. Let's have some drinks before dinner," Mica said, patting a chair next to him for Townsend to take.

Ben hadn't noticed the man in full livery until Mica mentioned drinks. He seemed to have popped out of thin air, a silent genie waiting to do the bidding of the master. Ben remembered that Roberta, their guide, had told them *The Loyalty* had a servant crew of fifteen who stayed aboard on a permanent basis. The man took their orders without using a pencil or pad. He smiled at everything and nodded his head. Somehow, Ben knew that he wouldn't miss a thing.

"I understand you had quite a day," Townsend said to Karen, patting her hand in a fatherly way.

"It was horrible."

"If it weren't for Link, I'd be being fitted for a jewel in my navel and a harem skirt right now," Coco told him.

Link brushed her words aside. "Let's not forget Mr. Kane's bravery. I dropped in with a small army. Ben was going to save the ladies with his bare hands."

Karen looked at Ben admiringly. "And he would have, too," she said. "Unfortunately, Greta gave him away."

"Let's just say I was happy as hell to see Link and his band of merry men," Kane said.

The waiter deposited their drinks unobtrusively, and melted away to the side as Link told Dr. Townsend about the rescue on Pelican Island.

Ben took a sip of his vodka and wondered if he should light his cigar. Lord Phillip Carlisle, Crown Commissioner of the British Virgin Islands—and Ben's worthy opponent in chess—had given him a cache of Havana Presidentes. He opted to wait until after dinner.

"You said you got involved because of Kalaxis?" Ben prodded.

Mica nodded. "That's right. My Greek friend was supposed to be a patient on Mica Island. When I heard that he and his crew had been murdered, I vowed to avenge his death," Mica said solemnly.

"How did you find them on Pelican Island?" Ben asked.

Link balanced his glass in his hand, as if debating how much information he should reveal. "Ben, have you ever heard of SARSAT?"

Ben thought about it. "It's some kind of satellite network, isn't it?"

"Right. The name stands for Search and Rescue Satellites. It's one of the few areas where the United States and Russia maintain cooperation. What it does is monitor the earth for distress calls, using satellites as monitors on emergency frequencies. Russia has three satellites in the SARSAT system, and the U.S. has another three. Between those six, and two others from Canada, there's a complete blanketing of the earth's surface. If a ship goes down in the water, or a plane hits the drink, SARSAT is supposed to pinpoint the position."

"Okay, but how did that help you?" Kane asked.

"We found the boat where the German girls were taken from, and we had Kalaxis' yacht. That gave me coordinates to work from. I tapped into the SARSAT system and modified the data to find out what communications came over the air at those coordinates."

"You were able to access the computers of the United States and Russia?"

"The Soviet Union's were child's play. I know at least ten thirteen-year-old hackers who could crack their codes. The U.S. codes are more sophisticated, but I had an advantage."

"Really?" said Karen.

"I invented them. So now I got a printout of the distress call in both of the areas where the empty yachts were found. In both cases, they sent out calls for help about a small fishing boat on fire. I had my engineers man their listening posts and scan the airwaves for anyone calling in with a fire emergency."

"Couldn't you just use the SARSAT system?" Coco asked him.

"Good question. The problem was, it takes a while to unscramble the codes. You have to kiss a lot of toads before you get a prince. It was a hell of a lot easier to wait for the next distress call."

"What happened then?" Karen asked, listening intently to Mica's explanation.

"Well, we picked up Nancy's Mayday call, and then the response from Mr. Kane and his person on Barracuda Reef."

"Sure, but by the time I got to the *Elgin*, it was too late," Ben said.

"Right, but we were able to intercept a message from the fishing boat to the copter station," Mica said. "I got the whole conversation. The fishing boat says we got two more and send the chopper over, and the mother ship says fine, bring them over to Pelican and we'll be along in a little while. The rest is history," Mica said, with a smile.

"Very impressive," Kane acknowledged. "What happened to the mother ship?"

"Major Frank, who's in charge of the Mica Security Forces, staged a raid simultaneously with ours on a yacht named the *Crimson Star*. They rounded up a Libyan student, two Palestinians wanted by Interpol, and a Moroccan businessman who had been arrested previously on white slavery charges. The Palestinians revealed the whole scheme. It seems this gang had high-up connections in the Moroccan government. The authorities are making arrests as we speak."

"Thank God someone else won't have to go through what we did," Coco said.

"That's right," Karen agreed.

"Link," Dr. Townsend said, "you never cease to amaze me."

"Well, then, let me continue to amaze you with the culinary delights prepared in our galley." On cue, the waitress appeared and began serving.

"I hope you weren't in the mood for anything exotic," Mica said. "I can't stand the food around here. They've got this *fungii* which is really a cornmeal paste, and turtle soup, and the worst damn ice cream called *soursop*. Who wants to eat a meal composed of things like *fungii* and *soursop*? So I decided to bring the good old USA to the Virgins."

Mica had disregarded the fact that the Virgin Islands were already part of the USA, and Ben didn't bring it up.

They began with chilled fruit cup, and then were served their choice of turkey, roast beef, or steak, all prepared in a way that pleased the eye as well as the palate. They finished off with a choice of rich desserts, including strawberry shortcake, chocolate cheesecake, or orange sherbet. It was a very enjoyable dinner, and Link Mica proved himself to be an excellent host.

It was obvious also that Coco had her eyes on the billionaire industrialist. She laughed at his every joke and hung on to his every word.

Through the course of the evening, Kane learned a lot about Link Mica. Townsend seemed to idolize him, and talked about Link's early years. From what the scientist said, and from Link's own recollections, Ben was able to piece together Mica's story.

Link had grown up in rural Montana in a middle-class family. His father had been a postal worker and his mother a teacher at the local high school. The young Mica wasn't much of a student. In fact, he was left back in the sixth grade, much to the embarrassment of his mother, for cutting class. In high school the situation grew even worse. Link was basically a loner, content to putter around with electronics and read science magazines.

At the age of eighteen, he built his own computer. To hear Townsend tell it, he used bicycle parts and tin cars. A year later, he developed a computer that was more powerful and cheaper to make than anything else on the market. He launched the Mica I computer line, borrowing money from friends and taking a loan from the local bank. The Mica I achieved incredible success. Link became an overnight sensation, and turned down lucrative offers to buy out his fledgling company. Instead he went public, made his first million, and turned the day-to-day operation of the business over to professional managers.

Link then began a software company and devoted his energies to two areas. He saw a need in the future for governments and corporations to protect their hard data, so he devised ingenious security devices to protect access to data banks. The other area he was involved with was artificial intelligence, particularly voice recognition. His Micasoft Company garnered over a third of the market, and once again Link resisted overtures to sell. He followed the same pattern as he had with Mica I, but this time amassed fifty million and controlling interest.

Financial magazines began labeling his business acumen as the "Mica Touch" because anything he touched seemed to turn to gold. His next three ventures were in the fields of gene splicing, Mica-tech, chemicals, Micatron; and cosmetics, Mica-care. Each of these companies spun off their own subsidiaries, and eventually, Link combined his whole operation under the flag of Mica Industries.

He had done all this before his twenty-eighth birthday.

"The secret is in hiring good people. You can't be afraid to take a chance, and if you have a question about something, go to the best person around and let him answer it for you," Mica told them.

"You make it sound so easy," Coco said, "as if any one of us could do it."

"Anyone *can* do it. Of course, if you want to keep on top of things, you've got to devote your life to it. I've missed a few things along the way. I have no personal life to speak of."

"But you do have friends," Karen said to him.

"There are people who are friendly to me, but I don't know if you could call them *friends*. My business takes me all over the world, so there's not much time to socialize. I need more than an office, so I created *The Loyalty*. Most of the time I just sail into a port, take care of a problem with one of the corporations, and then sail on to the next problem."

Dr. Townsend grinned. "Just remember what Malcolm Forbes said: 'The wealthy are always complaining about the burden of wealth, but you never see them trying to share the burden.'"

Link threw his head back and laughed. "Very good, Robert."

"Anyone mind if I smoke?" Kane asked, pulling the Havana out of his pocket.

Coco looked as if she might object, until she saw Link Mica's reaction.

"That looks like a Presidente,' Mica remarked.

"You're on the money. Straight out of Havana into a humidor."

"I used to love those," Mica said, shaking his head.

Kane fished out another from his pocket and handed it to Link. "Be my guest."

Link beamed his appreciation. "Much obliged. I'll save it for a special celebration."

Karen fidgeted with her napkin. She had been waiting for the right time to ask Link and Townsend something, and this seemed as good as any.

"Link, Robert, maybe you can explain something to me. You know, I'm going to be working on Mica Island in a couple of days. I'm not sure I completely understand the need to stay incommunicado for three months. I imagine it's important that the patients see a continuity of staff, and I know that emergency situations occur and you'd want the staff person assigned to be there, but . . ."

"It's more than that, Karen," Townsend said with a benevolent smile. He looked over at Mica for some direction.

Link leaned back in his chair. "Karen, The Facility is one of the most exclusive places in the world. Every bit of its exterior and interior has been well thought out for optimum effect in making the patient well. For example, you will see that most of the colors in The Facility are yellow and powder blue, since Robert tells me those are the colors that enable people to respond better to behavioral modification. The menus are planned with an eye toward optimal benefit for the patient. In The Facility, we will regulate the environment as much as is humanly possible, twenty-four hours a day. We even require the patients to sleep with a set of headphones that play white noise for the soundest sleep possible."

"It's a concept, Karen," Townsend explained, "that stimulates beta waves in the brain and enables the patient to accept the personality changes we are asking of him or her."

"Those are all wonderful reasons for the patients to be locked up on the island, but why the staff?"

Mica and Townsend laughed.

"Believe me, Karen, you won't consider yourself locked up," Townsend explained patiently. "It is a paradise. Every need is provided for. We've had both staff and patients beg us to let them stay longer. I've been personally offered fortunes if I would let a particular patient stay even one day extra."

"You'll find that your patients are among the wealthiest and most powerful people in the world," Link told her.

"Yes," Townsend agreed, "and that's the problem. The fact is, the world is shaped and molded by a relatively small handful of talented, wealthy, and powerful people. Perhaps there are five thousand men and women who truly shape the course of history. They may be the great writers, or actors, or politicians, or inventors. These are the people who can make the world, through their thoughts and actions, a better place for all mankind."

"We cater to these elite," Link Mica said. "They don't have to spend a penny to be accepted, either."

"For the good of mankind, we cannot waste the minds of these people because of alcohol, drugs, or any other kind of addiction. That is the philosophy of The Facility."

Townsend continued, "Link has provided the

best security in the world around Mica Island, for a very good reason. If, for some reason, the names of the people who came to The Facility were ever made public, it would mean the end of those people and their ability to wield the influence they have. If we were treating the Pope for heroin addiction—which by the way we're not," Townsend grinned—"how do you think that would go over in the parishes around the world? Or what if you had a general in charge of a nuclear arsenal and the word got out that he was gambling addict being treated at The Facility? In no time, he'd be out of his job and someone else would take his place."

Coco shrugged. "Maybe that's not such a bad idea."

"Well, it is, because we can help this general to beat his addiction and maintain his level of performance. If his problems went untreated, he could become a threat to world peace. But in order to help these people, absolute security is vital."

"So you want me to stay without contact from the outside world to protect the identity of the patients?" Karen asked.

"Precisely!"

"What's to stop me from telling the world once I leave? What's to stop any of the patients from talking about their famous colleagues?"

"To do so would only reveal to the world that they, too, were patients. It's not in their interests to do so. And we have another method to insure secrecy. Dr. Townsend has devised a method that seems to work well."

Townsend shrugged. "It's nothing more than posthypnotic suggestion, amplified by the use of some new chemical discoveries from the Micatron people. Thus far, we've been successful in preserving our patients' anonymity. I hope it will continue."

Karen looked at Kane and shrugged. "I guess that is the best way to maintain control."

"Who selects these people?" Kane wanted to know.

"Once again, in the interests of security, only I know the people who apply for treatment," Link told him. "I check out each person through discreet channels and decide on his or her eligibility. It's not a foolproof system, but I think it's worked very well so far."

Townsend said enthusiastically, "Karen, you will be amazed when you see the rate of success. It is beyond my wildest imaginings. It must have to do with the surroundings and the nearly laboratory-perfect control of the environment."

"Almost makes me upset that I don't have some kind of addiction just so I could join your summer camp," Kane said, flicking the ash off his cigar.

CHAPTER 7

Jacob Peters shook hands with his two bunkmates and threw his three white T-shirts and two pairs of cutoff jeans into his duffel bag. He left the Mica uniforms on his bed. He had agreed in the original contract that the uniforms must stay on the island when his three months of work were completed.

He checked the little pocket calendar he had kept on the wall and smiled with satisfaction at all the X's he had crossed through the dates with his red marking pencil. Today, the last day, he had written in and circled the name Sharon, using the same red marker. He sighed deeply and reached into his pocket for the picture he kept of his fiancée.

"You're going to wear that picture away to a frazzle," Billy Thomas said, laughing and slapping him on the back.

"I never get tired of looking at her," Jacob said solemnly.

"Is that what you're going to do when you see her tonight after three months on this island?" Paul Wendell asked him with a big gap-toothed grin. "You just going to sit and stare at her?"

"Never mind what I'll be doing tonight,' Jacob scolded.

There was a knock on Jacob's door. Little John opened it a crack and looked in.

"Hey, mon, Mrs. Baxter wants to see you in the Administration Building right away," he told Jacob.

"Thank you, Little John," Jacob called out.

He was wondering when they would call for him. They would have to arrange for a boat or a chopper to take him back to St. Thomas.

He walked down the neatly landscaped paths, past the statues and the spouting fountains, until he came to the round white marble building bearing the green-and-red flag and the Mica rock M logo.

He smiled at the guard at the door, not expecting any response. The people in the Mica Security Forces were called "the machines" because they never spoke or acted the least bit human. After a while you got used to their stone-cold faces and lifeless eyes, especially when everyone else was so friendly.

Mrs. Baxter's office was on the second floor. He walked up the main stairs and said hello to the girl who worked in Mrs. Baxter's outer office.

"How are you, Jacob?" she asked him.

"Couldn't be better," he told her. "Going home today to see my woman. I've come to see Mrs. Baxter about the arrangements."

"Let me buzz her." She pressed a button on the desk. "It's Mr. Peters to see you."

A green light flashed over the door.

The girl smiled. "She can see you now."

He opened the door and walked in. Mrs. Baxter was sitting behind her desk. She was a reasonably attractive woman of around forty, with soft brown hair. She got up when she saw him, and extended her hand. On the wall behind her were several pictures of Link Mica.

"Jacob, how are you?"

"I'm fine, Mrs. Baxter. Just fine."

"Good, I'm so pleased to hear that. Won't you have a seat?"

She motioned for him to take the chair opposite her desk.

Jacob had seen her around The Facility during the course of his three months. She was usually talking to one of the guests, or inquiring at the Staff Social Building about one of the people she had hired. Whenever she saw him, she went out of her way to walk over and say hello.

"I just want you to know, Jacob, that we're very

pleased with the way you have done your job here in the last three months. I send personal reports from the supervisors over to Mr. Mica himself, and I had the occasion to talk to Roberta, Mr. Mica's personal secretary, who told me that Link felt the Food Staff was doing a super job."

"We have good people in Food," Jacob told her.

"Good people are working all over the island."

"Yes, that's very true," Jacob agreed.

She picked up a file and Jacob saw that his name was typed on the label. She thumbed through some of the pages, which he guessed were reports by his supervisors on him. He had always gotten along well with the supervisors and found them to be fair.

"I'm going to ask you a few questions, Jacob."

"All right."

"Have you been happy working here?"

"Oh, yes. It's the very best job I ever had."

Mrs. Baxter smiled at him. "Jacob, you don't know how happy that makes me feel," she said warmly. "Was there anyone or anything that gave you any trouble over the last three months? Please let me know, because we want everything to be just right for the staff at The Facility."

Jacob thought it over. "I can't think of anything."

"Excellent. I'm recommending that you get a ten-percent raise, and as of today, you get your own room."

Jacob wasn't following what she was saying.

"Excuse me?"

"I said a ten-percent raise. Don't thank me, you earned it."

She reached into the drawer of her desk and drew out a sheaf of papers. The papers looked like the original contract he had signed. She handed them over to him and gave him a pen.

"You can take your time and read it, if you like. It's the same contract you had last time for three months, but with the new provisions for the raise and the private room."

"I don't understand," Jacob said, looking down at the papers blankly.

"What don't you understand?"

"I don't want to work another three months. I want to go home."

Mrs. Baxter looked shocked. "Why, Jacob, what do you mean?"

"I worked my three months, and now it's over. It is time for me to leave."

"But, you said you were happy."

"I was happy, but now I want to go back to St. Thomas."

He felt his voice rising but he didn't care. He handed the contracts back to her.

"But what about The Facility? Don't you realize who these guests are? These are the most important people in the world."

"The most important person in the world to me is my woman, waiting for me on St. Thomas. Now, I don't know what the problem is. My contract said three months and that's all I care to work here. Please make arrangements to get me back to St. Thomas."

Mrs. Baxter sank back in her chair and just stared at Jacob. She made a visible effort to regain her composure.

"Yes. Yes, of course."

She lifted up the folder again and thumbed through the pages. "Can I ask you another question?"

Jacob didn't answer.

"When you sleep at night, do you use the headphones in order to get a restful sleep?"

They always made such a big fuss about the headphones. They were plugged into a socket over each bed and you were supposed to put them on when you went to sleep. The supervisors were constantly asking if you had the headphones on at night.

Paul and Billy thought it was stupid at first, but when they tried it, they found they really did get a better sleep and that it gave them a pleasant feeling when they woke up in the morning. They said they were more relaxed and happy during the day when they wore the headphones at night.

Jacob had worn the phones a couple of nights, but he had gotten an earache and he attributed it to the phones. He didn't wear them again, although he told the supervisors he always wore them.

"I wore them a couple of times."

"You're supposed to wear them every night."

"To tell you the truth, Mrs. Baxter, the damn things gave me an earache so I stopped using them."

"They can't give you an earache!" she snapped. Her face turned angry. She pressed a button on her desk. "I'll need someone to take Mr. Peters to the Security Building. He doesn't want to renew his contract," she said.

"I'm not going to the damn Security Building."

The door opened and two of the green-uniform-clad security men stood at the door.

"Go with them, Peters." Mrs. Baxter said. "They'll take care of you."

The two guards, each about six feet tall and carrying a drawn pistol, approached Jacob.

"Hey, what the hell is going on here?" Jacob asked.

"You could have made it all so easy," Mrs. Baxter said. "All you had to do was wear the damn headphones. Why couldn't you follow the rules, Peters?"

The guards grabbed him by the shoulders and lifted him out of his chair.

He pushed their hands off him, and they grabbed him even more roughly.

"The choice is up to you, Mister," the guard on his right said. "We can take you with us conscious or unconscious." He pulled out a blackjack and passed it in front of Jacob Peters' eyes.

"What's it going to be?"

CHAPTER 8

Lord Phillip Carlisle waved hello to his friend Ben Kane from the terrace of Windsor House. The sprawling white building, the seat of power of the British government on Tortola, was home to both Lord Carlisle and his daughter, Jessica Spencer Carlisle.

During the war, Lord Phillip had served as a commander of a Royal Navy corvette, the *Bramble*, and sailed the waters off the Virgin Islands. He never forgot the turquoise water and the lush green countryside. After many years of service to the Wilson government, Lord Carlisle, OBE, ME, received his peerage and was appointed to the post of Crown Commissioner of the British Virgin Islands as a form of honorable retirement. Approaching seventy, Lord Phillip was still a very savvy man who didn't mind people thinking him an old-school Englishman put out to pasture in the balmy tropics.

He had become friends with Ben Kane after a chess tournament between the U.S. Virgins and the British Virgins. They enjoyed their match so much that they continued the series on their own. By now, Kane had two games on Lord Phillip, but the Crown Commissioner was certain he'd be able to launch a comeback.

Lord Phillip knew that, aside from their chess game, another reason for Kane's visits to Windsor House was to see Jessica. His daughter had arrived from England two years ago after a disastrous marriage ended in divorce. He had suggested she get a change of scenery from London and spend some time with him. He was quite worried about his tall, blond, seemingly unflappable daughter. Her business-obsessed, philandering husband had been the talk of the East End social circles for months.

It was almost uncanny the way Jessica reminded Phillip of her mother. She immediately got busy and assumed the role that her mother had fulfilled in her lifetime, that of social directrix of the BVI's upper crust. She organized Lord Phillip's entertaining and ran his household. Looking back, he couldn't understand how he had ever been able to muddle through without her.

She was introduced to Ben Kane during the first week of her stay, and Phillip wondered how important that meeting was in changing Jessica's ideas about returning to England. He, of course, was quite happy that his daughter wanted to stay with him.

"Good of you to come, Ben," he said, shaking the American's hand.

"Good of you to invite me," Kane replied.

Lord Phillip walked Ben into the dark-wood-paneled den and poured him a glass of Absolut, and took a brandy for himself.

"I didn't see Jesse around," Kane said.

"She's off shopping, I'm afraid. She did know you were coming, and I'm sure she'll be by soon to say hello."

They were three moves into the game when Lord Phillip looked up at Ben. "By the way, old boy, did your friend Karen ever take that job on Mica Island? You know, the girl who was involved with the slavers."

Ben nodded. "Yes, she did. I saw her off this morning. She goes incommunicado now for the next three months."

"Hmmm," Lord Carlisle said noncommittally.

"Did you find out anything?"

When Karen had told Ben that she would be staying at The Facility for three months without being able to make or receive calls or send or receive mail, Ben had asked Lord Phillip to look into the place. From the look of Phillip Carlisle, Ben could see that his friend had some information.

"Come on, Lord Phillip. Out with it," Kane said good-naturedly.

"Not much to tell, really. When you mentioned Mica Island it rang a bell, you know, because my late wife's brother spent some time there. I couldn't say anything to you then, old chap. Hope you understand that I had to check with Reggie first, make sure he had no objections, and all that."

"Reggie?"

"Yes, Colonel Reginald Thornton, R.A.F."

"Then he had an addiction of some kind?"

"Painkillers. He was shot down over Germany, I'm afraid, and the Nazis wanted to know a bit about his squadron. They tortured him, and I think he started with codeine so he could sleep. Well, after a long while the pain went away, but he couldn't seem to stop the codeine addiction."

"So he went to The Facility for the cure?"

"Yes. I thought he might have some reservations about talking about it, but on the contrary, he was positively delighted. He had only good things to say about The Facility. He told me that he's off codeine and he feels that Dr. Townsend saved his life. He'd like to tell the whole world about Mica Island and the fine work they do there."

"No reservations?"

"None, as far as I could tell. He's on vacation

down here just now, and I've invited him for dinner. I do hope you can join us. Jessica would be very upset if you didn't."

"I think I would enjoy that very much. Thank you."

Reginald Thornton turned out to be a heavy-set, red-faced man with bushy gray eyebrows and an overbearing manner.

Jessica had seen to a perfectly prepared meal of fritters and prawn meat, black bean soup, and a pepper pot consisting of a highly seasoned stew of meat and peppers. Dessert was a colorful plate of tropical fruits.

Thornton complained that the soup was too cold, the pepper pot too hot, and that he had tasted better fruit.

Jessica and Phillip were obviously used to Reginald Thornton because neither of them got upset. They seemed to take his complaining in stride.

"What a bore!" Ben told Jessica, catching her alone for a moment when Uncle Reggie and her father adjourned to the billiard room.

"You can't take Uncle Reggie seriously, Ben. Actually, Father and I think he's rather funny. He's very important in England, you know. I believe he heads up the purchasing section in the Ministry of Defense."

"No wonder England is in such big trouble,"

Kane said.

"No, really. I hear he's quite good at what he does. He does most of his work by written correspondence and bids, so I suppose his personality isn't too much of a factor in the performance of his duties."

Jessica was wearing a simple blouse and skirt. Her jade necklace brought out the color of her beautiful blue-green eyes.

"You look lovely tonight, Jessica. I've missed you," Kane told her.

"It seems you've found someone else to keep you busy—this Karen whatever her name is."

"Why, Jessica, I never thought I'd see you jealous."

"My, how we do flatter ourselves," Jessica said, smiling. "Now, why don't you join the men in the billiard room. I'll stop by in a bit."

Lord Phillip offered Ben a cigar as Thornton leaned over the table and tried to sink the eight ball.

"I gave one of these to Link Mica," Ben told him, waiting for Reggie's reaction.

Thornton stroked the cue ball solidly and the eight popped into the side pocket. "Oh, have you met Link?"

"I was on his yacht," Ben said.

"Quite a chap. I was very taken with him."

Thornton lined up the three ball and decided he needed a bridge to make the shot.

"Lord Phillip tells me that you were at The Facility."

"I was." This time the tip of his cue glanced off the ball and the three wouldn't drop. "Where did you get such a miserable table? That shot should have gone in."

"Sorry," Phillip said coolly. He leaned over the table and knocked in the three, and then ran off another six balls before he paused to take a sip of his sherry.

"They treat addiction. Whatever the addiction is, they work on it," Reggie said. "Dr. Robert Townsend is head of staff. The man's an absolute genius. We had gambling addicts, drug addicts, alcohol, of course, even people addicted to food. Personally, I had a bit of a problem with codeine."

"Would I know some of the other people who shared in this miracle with you?" Kane asked.

"I don't know, and I don't think I would tell you if I did. Some people need to have their privacy. Oh, good, Phillip, you finally missed." Thornton chalked his cue and surveyed the table.

Phillip had played it safe, not leaving Thornton any clear shots.

"When you arrive," Thornton continued, "they make you sign a paper agreeing to be hypnotized for security reasons. I know there were other people with me on the island, but because of the hypnosis, I can't remember them."

"How do they work this cure?" Ben asked him.

"Well, there's not much magic to it. They have trained people who talk to you. You sit in on groups and get individual counseling. They give you these drugs that Dr. Townsend discovered, some kind of megavitamin compound, and you get a good night's sleep."

"It doesn't seem that much more radical than many other clinics."

"They never say the word 'clinic,' it's always 'The Facility,'" Thornton corrected.

Thornton ran out the rack and waited for Phillip to set up the next game. He balanced his weight on the cue stick and looked at Kane. "You know, another American chap was asking me questions about The Facility. The fact is, you remind me of him in a small way."

"Really?"

"Yes. He wanted to know as much as possible about the place. I met him on the golf course and we started up a conversation. Maybe you know him." He patted his shirt and then his pants. "I think he gave me his card. Here, do you know him?"

The simple business card read "C. Weaver, Ultratech" in raised black letters. It belonged to a man Kane knew very well.

Kane had known Weaver since his days in Vietnam. Even then, the man with the close-cropped blond hair and steel-gray eyes had been manipulating Ben Kane and his men.

Weaver had worked for CORDS, Civil Operations and Revolutionary Development Support. Under Weaver's orders, Kane found himself ferrying operatives and taking part in shadowy missions which made no sense to him but which Weaver insisted figured prominently in "the big picture." Weaver had an enormous amount of clout in the Saigon theater, so Ben and his crew did what they were told and didn't ask questions.

But things had changed since the war. Kane had his own fleet, and Weaver was working for the same "company" but under the Ultratech cover in the Caribbean. Their paths crossed from time to time, usually when Weaver needed to use the contacts and fleet Kane had built up throughout the islands. Only now, Kane could pick and choose the missions.

"I wonder what Weaver's stake is in all this," Lord Phillip mused out loud, breaking into Kane's thoughts.

"He probably has some problem that needs correcting. I told the man he should get in touch with them," Thornton said.

"I don't think Weaver has any human vices, Colonel. Sometimes I wonder if Weaver is human at all," Kane said.

Jessica stepped into the room. "Mind if a woman comes into this male lair?"

"By all means, my dear," Lord Phillip said, kissing his daughter on the cheek. "Perhaps Uncle Reggie would play you a game. She's quite good, you know."

"No, thank you," Thornton said in a clipped tone. "I don't play pocket billiards with females."

"Umm, quite so," Lord Phillip said, giving Jessica an exasperated look.

"Will you be staying over, Uncle Reggie? There's a beastly storm outside, and Lord knows we have the room."

"No, thank you, my dear. I have to be back at the hotel."

"What about you, Kane?" Phillip asked. "No sense going back to the Reef in this storm. Might as well wait it out till morning."

Kane sneaked a look at Jessica. She was purposely avoiding his eyes, he thought.

"Why, thank you, Lord Phillip. I think I will take you up on your offer. Perhaps we could get another game of chess in before you retire so I can get a chance to stay two up on you."

"My pleasure, old man."

CHAPTER 9

Mike Mulhaney watched the rain come down in torrents from the doorway of his Rainbow Keg.

Over forty years ago Mulhaney had plunked down the little money he had and purchased the Navy dock yard facilities and the land of Barracuda Reef. With the postwar tourist boom, Mulhaney found himself a land baron being offered millions for the out-of-the-way private harbor.

The years had put some weight on the ex-PC boat officer, and his beard, once black as coal, had become as white as Santa's. A mild heart attack had slowed him down a bit further, and instead of spending fifteen hours a day supervising the dock yards, he gave the day-to-day operation of running the yard to his daughter Michelle, while he presided over his Rainbow Keg tavern.

Chief Bukowski and Ganja Grant were sitting at their customary table talking about Kane and what had gone down the other day at Pelican Cove. Mike brought over a bottle of rum and refilled all their glasses.

He was a bit lonely, he decided. Michelle was away in Florida on business, trying to buy a power winch. As much as he argued with her about his drinking or smoking too much, he missed his only child.

"So where is that boss of yours?" he asked them.

"The commander is off to Tortola visiting Lord Phillip," Bukowski told him.

"Another one of those chess matches?" Mike asked.

"He's hoping Lord Phillip could use some of his sources and get some information on this Mica Island."

"What's the problem with Mica Island? From what I read in the papers, this Link Mica seems to be a pretty decent guy. He's looking to spend his millions helping people, and there are sure too few of those kind around today."

"Ben was wondering why a guy like that needs a high-power strike force, I guess," Chief Bukowski said, shaking his head.

Mike took another swig of his rum. "If he had any brains, he'd stay over tonight. Looks like a damn hurricane out there, even though I didn't hear any prediction for one."

Ganja pushed his rum back over to Mulhaney. "Got to stay clean, my man," he said.

"Oh, pardon me, Your Holiness," Mike said, giving Bukowski a wink. "I forgot you never touch the devil's brew."

Chief picked up his glass and downed the rum in one gulp. "You'll do a lot better drinkin' this, son, than smokin' that weed you're so fond of."

"Different strokes, man, . . ." Ganja told him.

"Speaking of poison, where's your third musketeer?"

"Miles'll be around soon enough, Mike. He had to lock up the office tonight. We had a couple of charters out in this storm and Miles wanted to be sure we got them in safely before we closed up for the day," Bukowski said.

"I saw you had another reporter in this morning from *Yacht World*," Chief mentioned to Mulhaney.

"Yeah. They come out of the woodwork this time of year. They all think they're doin' me some kind of big favor. 'I'll put your Reef on the map,' he says to me. The damn fool doesn't know that I've spent a good part of my life making sure it doesn't get on the map."

"How long can you keep squashing the stories?" Ganja asked him.

"As long as there are editors willing to take a little under the table. Right, Mike?" Bukowski said.

"You're not far from wrong, Chief," Mike agreed solemnly. "Ahh, to hell with them! Have another to wet your whistle, Chief, and I'll get our choirboy here some soda pop."

As Mike started to get up, he saw Miles and an Island woman walk into the Keg. "Do my eyes deceive me, or is that Miles with a woman?"

The thin quiet man was removing his rain slicker and hanging it on the hook to the right of the door.

The young, attractive woman handed him her coat and shook out her hair by running her hands through it. She was a light-skinned black woman in her early twenties.

"She's not bad," Mike said.

"I think I know her," Ganja told him.

Miles told the woman to wait, and walked over to the table.

"The lady came over to the office and says she knows you, Ganja. Her name is Sharon, and she—"

"She's the nurse from St. Thomas Hospital," Ganja said suddenly. "What the hell is she doing here?"

Miles shrugged. "She wouldn't tell me. She said she had to speak to you. Something personal."

"Uh, oh! I think I better be startin' to knit a baby blanket," Bukowski kidded.

"I got a couple of booties upstairs I can loan

you," Mike told him.

Ganja wasn't paying any attention. His eyes were riveted on the woman. She was trying to smile, although it was obvious that she was deeply troubled about something. Ganja walked over to her and took her to a quiet table, away from the rest of the people.

"I didn't know if you'd recognize me, Ganja," she said in a quiet voice.

"You don't forget someone who saved your life," Ganja said. "What brings you all the way over here on such a night?"

"Well, my mother lives here, and I was staying with her. Then I remembered that you worked on Barracuda Reef. I thought perhaps you could help me."

The flood of tears that she had tried for so long to hold back finally broke through. Ganja picked up a napkin and helped her to dry her eyes.

"Now you tell old Ganja what the problem is and I'm sure we can straighten it out."

"You see, I don't have anyone to turn to. You did tell me . . ."

"That's right! I said if you ever have a problem, you come to the Ganja man. Now, you cry it out and then we'll see how we can help you."

Ganja remembered her from St. Thomas Hospital. He had been doing some diving and there had been an accident with the moorings. The next thing he knew, the diving bell was dropping out of control. Somehow he had fought his way to the surface, but his body was ravaged by the bends. Sharon Marcy had saved his life by her proficiency with the hospital's decompression chamber.

Ganja waited for her to stop crying. He asked her if she wanted a drink and she shook her head no.

"Do you remember I told you about Jacob?" she finally said.

"Dude you were going to be marry? What happened?"

She told him the story of how Jacob and she had decided that he would work on Mica Island for three months so they would have enough money to get married and live in the house they both wanted.

"Well, what happened?" Ganja asked her gently.

"The people from Mica called me to say that he wouldn't be returning and that he'd signed up for another three months. I couldn't believe it, Ganja. It isn't like my Jacob. He would never do such a thing."

Ganja didn't say anything. He knew that people changed, and sometimes it could be painful.

"Maybe things will be better in three more months."

"No, Ganja. You don't understand. They did something to him to make him sign the contract."

"How do you know this?"

"I have proof. Look."

She handed Ganja a piece of paper that had been folded to less than a half inch. He carefully unfolded it and read what it said:

Dearest Sharon:

The days are endless but now there are only two left before I see you. I love you and can't wait till you are my wife.

J.P.

"How did you get this?"

"Jacob became friendly with another man in the food building where he stayed. This man became very ill and he couldn't work anymore. They decided to transfer him to the St. Thomas Hospital. When Jacob found this out, he asked the man to carry a message to me because he knew he would be at my hospital. I received this note yesterday, the same day Jacob signed on for another three months. I believe they are holding him there against his will."

"Can you stay here tonight? I want you to show this to my friend, Ben Kane. He has someone on Mica Island and I'm sure he will be very interested in everything you have to say.

"I'll ask Mike Mulhaney to put you up in one of his rooms upstairs. Ben Kane will be back tomorrow morning. Don't worry, Sharon. We'll find out what's going down." Ganja took her hand and gave it a reassuring pat.

"Thank you, Ganja," she said. She covered her face with her hands and sobbed silently.

CHAPTER 10

Karen finished her dinner and left the Psychology Staff Building to take a walk around the grounds.

She had been reading the case histories of the patients at the facility, and what she read left her greatly disturbed. Dr. Townsend had dropped off the thirty or so folders and asked her to give him her opinion in a few days. She had become so engrossed by what she had read that she finished all of the cases in a few hours. She would have to tell Robert what she thought, but she wasn't looking forward to it.

All her life she had dreamed about working with

a man of Dr. Townsend's stature, and now she was going to have to confront him on the very first day.

She marched up to Dr. Townsend's cottage and knocked on the door. All the senior staff members lived in spotless white cottages near the center of the Facility. The other staff people lived dorm style in modern buildings resembling resort hotels. Her own cottage was just as big as the home she'd left back in the States. When she'd first opened the door, she'd found a huge sign welcoming her to The Facility from Townsend and the rest of the staff. Link Mica had sent a beautiful set of crystal glasses as a housewarming present.

At first, when Robert didn't answer, she thought he must be out. Then she remembered that the octogenarian was getting to be hard of hearing. She knocked louder, and this time she heard his footsteps as he approached the door.

"Oh, Karen, hello. Please come in."

She followed him into the cottage and then into the living room. The room was filled with books from floor to ceiling. Some of the books, half opened with place marks, covered the sofa and the table.

"Please excuse the mess. I don't have company often, and I keep forgetting to put things back once I've taken them out. I guess it's a habit one gets into after living alone for half a century."

Karen lifted a heavy tome from the sofa and handed it to Townsend. He looked at the cover, nodded, and placed it on the table in the kitchen.

"I was looking for that one yesterday," he told her.

He saw the case histories she was carrying under her arm. "Don't tell me you've finished them already,' he said.

"Yes, I have."

"What do you think of them?" he asked her.

"They're very interesting," she said.

"Umm hmm. I'm going to make myself some coffee. Would you like a cup? It won't take but a moment, it's instant." He walked into the kitchen.

"No, thank you."

"What were you saying about the cases?" he called to her.

Karen chose her words carefully. "I said the cases were very interesting. In fact, the most interesting studies I've ever read."

Robert Townsend came out of the kitchen balancing a cup of coffee on a saucer. "So you were impressed."

"Very."

"Then why do you look like there's something you're holding back from me?"

"I don't want to hurt your feelings," she told him.

Townsend shrugged. "Maybe you will, maybe you won't. Why don't you tell me what's on your mind and let me worry about my feelings."

"Okay." Karen took a deep breath. "These case histories are evidence of the greatest program in the history of behavioral science, or . . . a crock of shit."

Townsend nodded. "Go on."

"You've got people who've been lifelong alcoholics and they're cured in six to seven days. You've got shoplifters, and kleptos, and pyromaniacs, and compulsive gamblers, nymphomaniacs, and every kind of garden variety addict, including cigarette fiends who smoke four to five packs a day. And every one of them gets cured in a week to ten days.

"And how do you cure them? I'm looking for some significant breakthrough so I can make some kind of rationalization as to the miracles that are taking place at this facility, but . . . there's nothing! It's the same techniques of role model, positive reinforcement, alternative behavior, all building up self-image. Come on, Robert. That type of basic psychological therapy has never achieved a success ratio like you have in these histories."

Townsend sipped his coffee and didn't say anything.

"Why are you allowing yourself to be used in this charade? Is Link Mica behind these lies?" she said, holding up the files.

"No," he said. "Are you sure you won't have a cup of coffee?"

"Robert, have you been listening to me?"

"Yes, I have, Karen. That's one of the reasons I wanted you here with me. I need someone I can trust, someone who isn't afraid to say what she thinks, even if it is to a Nobel Prize–winner with many years in the field."

"Robert, tell me what's going on," she said quietly.

"I don't know. I honestly don't know. You see, those reports disturb me as much as they do you. I'm disturbed for a different reason. You're upset because you think they're all lies. I'm upset because I know that they're all true."

"You're joking!"

"No. Everything you read there happened. Nicotine addicts have thrown away their cigarettes and haven't the slightest desire. Lifelong alcoholics are completely cured. The same with every other category. And I'm at a loss to explain why.

"At first, I thought that Link was setting me up with phony patients. I had no idea why he would do that, but it was the only rational explanation I could think of. Then I recognized some of the people I was dealing with. There was a writer who I knew was a patient of a colleague of mine. This writer couldn't last two hours without a drink. After a few days here, he was stone-cold sober, and remained that way for weeks until he left."

"If you're telling me the truth, then there's another factor at work here that we don't recognize. Could it be something in the food?"

"No, I've had that checked. I also give them large doses of megavitamins. But I've been doing that with my patients for years and I've never had one quarter of this success."

"The staff counselors, then?"

"They're good people, well trained and capable,

but—"

"Wait a second! How about the earphones that you're supposed to wear every night when you go to sleep? There's all kinds of written reminders about that all over the place."

"Just white noise, Karen, to help people sleep and get good rest. The sounds stimulate beta waves in the brain and put the patient in a relaxed mood. Hospitals and clinics have been stimulating beta waves for over thirty years. I use it myself to get a good night's sleep. That can't be it."

"Subliminal messages?" Karen offered.

"There are no TVs or movies."

"Maybe it's just the total environment itself," Karen finally offered.

Townsend shrugged. "It's possible. This place is like the Garden of Eden. I just don't know. But I must confess that I feel like a bit of an ingrate. Here I have the dream of every therapist, a one-hundred-percent cure rate, and it's making me miserable, because I can't imagine how I'm achieving it."

Kane listened to what Ganja and the girl told him about Mica Island. He looked at the note that had been smuggled out, and tried to console the heartbroken young woman.

Ganja took her to the bus and told her to stay at her mother's until he contacted her.

He went back to the *Wu Li* to talk to Kane. "What do you think, Skipper?" he asked Ben.

Kane shrugged. "People get cold feet. Sometimes they need more time."

"Right," Ganja said, "but. . ."

Kane looked up at his friend.

"This isn't the first story I've heard like this," Ganja continued. "The Islanders are all talking about it. They say it's some kind of voodoo hex. Lots of people go over to work for Link Mica, but you don't hear about any of them coming back. Some cases, you can understand it, but there are other instances where it don't make no sense.

"You take Carter Woods. The man has six kids, most of them still in the house. Carter went over to Mica Island and didn't return. I never saw a man crazy about kids like Carter was for his. The reason he took the job in the first place was so that there'd be money for the kids to go to school. Now, how does it figure that he'd just sign up again without a word of explanation?"

"You have any ideas?" Kane asked him.

Ganja shrugged. "I would like to know what goes on in that place."

"Lord Phillip's brother-in-law swears by it," Kane told him. "He stayed a couple of weeks, got cured, and now is spreading the gospel according to Link Mica."

"I know that."

"But you still think that something is going on?"

"I wouldn't feel right if I didn't do what I could

for Sharon. She did save my life in that hospital."

"Well, I found out something. It seems our pal Weaver is also interested in what's going on. He made friends with Uncle Reggie Thornton, on the golf course no less, and was pumping him for information."

"You think he'd tell us anything?"

Kane shrugged. "It's worth a try."

He called the number of Ultratech in Charlotte Amalie and waited while the operator patched him through.

"Maybe we shouldn't be doing this," Ganja warned. "Any time we get mixed up with Weaver, we bite off more than we bargained for."

"You're right, Ganja. But right now Weaver is the only game in town. Mica is too big to be hassled by local authorities. If we want to get in on the inside, we need someone like Weaver to open the doors."

"Hello, Ben," Weaver said. His voice came in over the phone loud and clear. "What's doing, old buddy?"

"I need to talk to you," Ben said.

"I've always got time to meet with an old pal. Say, Ben, watch your patter. I'm out on the water and this is an open radio line. *Comprendez, amigo?*"

"When can I see you?" Kane asked him.

"Why don't you hop on out here this afternoon," Weaver offered. "I'm taking a little sun off the coast of St. John. Why don't you take a run over and we can meet at Red Beard's Bar on Coral Harbor. Around three o'clock? You know the spot?"

"Yes," Kane told him.

"Fine. I'll be looking forward to seeing you. *Ciao*." Weaver taking in the sun? Kane thought. He's got to be up to something.

Coral Harbor provided excellent anchorage. At the head of the bay, the dock had six feet of water. A marina and hauling facility were at the north of the dock, and east of it, in the mangroves, there was a channel with a full eight feet of water and a mud bottom, which provided excellent cover in bad weather . . . if you could survive the mosquitoes.

There was a grocery, Dave's Dive Shop, a few other small stores, including an Army/Navy store selling government surplus and a barber shop. Red Beard's Bar was a brick and mortar building painted a weatherbeaten red with a large wooden sign and a caricature of Red Beard painted on both sides.

Weaver was waiting at a table near the far wall. Like a gunfighter in the Old West, he always made sure his back wasn't exposed. He nodded slightly to Kane, his only concession to his presence, as he looked over the menu.

"I suggest the crayfish with a lemon sauce," Weaver advised.

"I'm not hungry," Kane said. "I'll just have an Absolut on the rocks."

Weaver was fastidious, as usual, in a white Stanley Blacker sports jacket and beige slacks. He wore a matching beige handkerchief in his breast pocket, and a beige-and-white Italian knit sweater. He signaled the waiter and ordered.

"So, to what do I owe this visit?" Weaver asked.

"Mica Island. The Facility. What do you know about it?" Kane responded.

"What makes you think I know anything about that place?"

"It's in your area, you've got to be curious," Kane told him.

"Curious about what? Link Mica is an American citizen. He's entitled to all the freedoms established in the Constitution. It isn't my job to spy on ordinary citizens."

The perennial cat-and-mouse game.

"Then how come you were nosing around Reggie Thornton?"

Weaver thought it over. "You're the one who had dinner with him on *The Loyalty* with Karen Aztec. Maybe I should be asking you."

"I thought you don't spy on ordinary citizens."

"I guess the key word here is 'ordinary,'" Weaver admitted. "I've heard that Miss Aztec is

98

on Mica's staff."

"You heard correctly. I'm concerned about her, Weaver. Particularly after what Ganja showed me."

"And what might that be?"

"I'll tell you if you're straight with me about why you're interested in the place."

"Why not." Weaver shrugged. "I'm not wild about the clientele, Kane old buddy. Over the past six months, we've had some of the most influential and powerful people in the world swim through our little fishbowl. That makes me nervous. You want to know what makes me even more nervous? A lot of these big shots weren't even from the Free World. We've had the heads of Commie governments, as well as left- and right-wing weirdos from all corners of the globe coming here."

"What do you know about the people who go to work on the island? Ganja tells me that there's a lot of Island people who never come back once they sign up."

"I've heard that kind of talk, too," Weaver said. "It's hard to know anything without someone on the inside."

"Come on, Weaver. You mean to tell me that you haven't put anyone in The Facility by now?"

"You know me better than that, Kane. Getting them in isn't the hard part."

"What's that supposed to mean?" Kane wanted to know.

Weaver shook his head. "Now it's your turn.

What is it that Ganja showed you that got you up in arms, old buddy?"

Kane showed him the note.

"The lady for whom that letter was intended tells me that it was written only a couple of days before her fiancé was to leave The Facility. He suddenly changed his mind and signed up for another three months. Doesn't that strike you as being odd?" Kane asked him.

"Ordinarily, I would say that things like that happen. But in the context of other things that are going on at Mica's Facility, I'm afraid it's par for the course."

He leaned close to Kane, even though there was no one else around. "What I'm going to tell you now is strictly confidential. I don't want any leaks on this one. Agreed?"

Kane nodded.

"I had a couple of my people infiltrate The Facility. These were trained experts with many years of service. They both knew the score, if you understand what I'm saying. Anyway, I lost them both," Weaver said, shaking his head.

"Killed?"

"No. They came back from a two-week stint and walked away from their jobs. They told me they were through with spook work and that it was counterproductive in benefiting mankind, or some such drivel, and they just walked out on me."

"What do you suspect? Drugs? Hypnosis?" Kane asked him.

"Hey, buddy boy, these agents represent a substantial investment by your Uncle Sam. We weren't about to let them become missionaries of a new world order without taking them apart and seeing what makes them tick. Guess what we found after we ran all the tests and analyzed all the data?"

"Nothing."

"Bingo. These dyed-in-the-wool A-1 operatives with sensitive security clearance were transformed in two weeks to mulch-spouting wimps loyal to Link Mica and the marvelous work he's doing in order to foster world peace."

"Doesn't say much for your operation," Kane said.

"Quite frankly, Kane, this Link Mica and the Facility scare the living shit out of me. We've routinely kept tabs on some of the most important people in America and world society, and let me tell you, Kane old buddy, all roads lead to Mica's mind spa."

"So what can we do about it? You can talk to people in Washington and call for an investigation, can't you?"

Weaver shook his head. "No way. Link Mica has clout that goes way up. I filed a couple of reports and was told to lay off. Officially, I'm out of it."

"But unofficially, you're willing to take some action on your own. Otherwise, you wouldn't be talking to me," Kane told him.

"Well, let's just say that you, as an independent contractor, might be able to accomplish something that I can't."

Weaver shrugged. "Here's what I can do for you, Kane. I can set you up with a phony identity. Do you remember Arthur Modesta?"

"He was a writer, wasn't he?"

"Right. He wrote the books that correctly predicted the economy for the seventies. He was acknowledged as a financial guru, and the world waited breathlessly for his next book. Which never materialized. Modesta took off to live on his farm in Oregon and no one has seen him since. That was ten years ago. He's about your age and build, and with the right kind of makeup, we can get you to pass for him and be invited to The Facility. Our problem is that Link knows you from your visit on *The Loyalty*."

"Townsend was there also."

"That makes it even more risky." Weaver made a face and shook his head. "No, let's drop that idea. It won't work."

Weaver chewed it over. "How about your man Ganja? I could set him up with a different name," Weaver mused. "He'd be a lot less risky, and could pass me information through you."

"What else can you do for us? If Ganja has a problem and has to abort, will you help?"

"I won't even know you, . . . never heard of you," Weaver said matter-of-factly.

"That's what I figured." Ben sighed. "Then it's up to Ganja. I'll let you know."

CHAPTER 11

Major Frank squeezed his six-foot, six-inch body into Link Mica's office chair and waited for the boss to come in. Frank had been Link's Chief of Security for three years now, and he knew that Link wanted to hear all the facts, even if it meant hearing news that wouldn't please him. And what he had to tell Link was definitely not going to please him.

It had taken the major ten minutes to get from The Facility to *The Loyalty*. During the ten minutes, he had thought of a dozen different ways to start the conversation and break the news to Mica.

Finally, he had settled on the most direct approach.

Link walked into the room wearing a terry cloth robe over his bright blue bathing trunks. He toweled off his hair as he sat down opposite Frank.

"You sounded as if you had something important to report, Major," Link said brusquely.

"Sir, your lady friend Miss Coco is a spy."

"Really?" Link's eyebrows went up. "On what do you base your assessment?" Link sounded annoyed.

"It's all in my report, sir." He handed Mica a dossier.

"Why don't you break it down for me, Major. I'll read it later."

"Very well. As you will remember, we had Mikhail Poteko, First Secretary of the KGB, as a guest. Mr. Poteko was good enough to inform us that Moscow had ordered him to place a mole in the Facility. The name of the operative was Anna Malik. She was sent first to Greece, where she was to be introduced to the shipping magnate Kalaxis. Kalaxis had already let people know he was going to be treated at The Facility. Anna Malik hoped to use Kalaxis to infiltrate and then report on her findings to Moscow. Anna Malik is Coco."

"You're sure that Coco and this Malik woman are the same?"

"Mikhail supplied us with fingerprints and pictures. The evidence is irrefutable."

Mica closed his eyes and leaned back in his

chair. He had become attached to the very pretty redhead. There was one thing, however, that he could never tolerate: Betrayal.

"You'll have to take her to The Facility and expose her to the correct thoughts," he told Frank sadly.

He should have known that Coco was too flexible, too eager to please. He was letting his guard down too much lately, leaving himself open for mistakes. He'd have to be more diligent in the future.

"Major, you have my sincere gratitude for your efforts."

"Shall I take her back with me now?"

"I'd like to talk to her first. She's on the ship somewhere. She shouldn't be too difficult to find."

Frank stood up and turned to the door in a quick military maneuver.

Alone for the first time in days, Coco walked below deck to the area where the guard was posted in front of the Communications Room.

She opened her purse and took out a compact. Very carefully, she unscrewed the back of her eyebrow pencil and removed one of the one-inch darts with the circumference of a straight pin. She made sure to hold the back as she took out two lipsticks. The lipsticks fitted perfectly, one on top of the other. The top case was the barrel, and the bottom case contained a charge of compressed air. One of the lipstick clasps was the trigger mechanism. She placed the dart into the barrel and walked into the hall, ten feet from the guard. He was staring straight ahead, his gun balanced in his hand.

She turned once, to be sure that no one was coming, then she pointed her sophisticated blowgun at the open spot between his ear and the bulge of his collarbone. The gun made a short hissing sound. At first she thought she had missed him. Then he shuddered, and collapsed to the floor. She moved quickly, getting another dart ready in case someone was inside the room.

Removing the electronic key card from the guard's belt, she unlocked the door and opened it slowly. A chair faced a sophisticated console filled with LED readout screens. There seemed to be no receiver in the room, just a very complicated transmitting apparatus hooked up to a mainframe computer.

Coco was wearing a gold pin in the shape of a leaf in her hair. She brought the pin to her eye and pressed down on the clasp. The well-disguised super-miniature camera could take up to thirty pictures with just the faintest light. Content that she had gotten everything, she once again opened the door.

The guard hadn't moved; the hall was completely clear. She closed the door behind her and stepped over his unconscious body.

The tranquilizer dart was a derivative of curare. When the guard woke up, he wouldn't be aware of the passage of time. For him, it would seem that he had closed his eyes for a second and woke up on the floor.

She made her way to the staircase and then to the stateroom cabin she was sharing with Link. The first chance she got, she would deliver the film to her contact on St. Thomas.

She didn't see Major Frank until it was too late. He stepped out from behind one of the suspended lifeboats and pushed her hard against the wall.

"What are you doing!" she said to him.

He didn't answer. He had a pistol in his hand and pressed it against her temple. He took her purse and pulled the gold leaf camera from her hair. "You won't be needing any of these things from now on," he said ominously. "We're going to see Link Mica. Don't give me an excuse to blow your head off. It's people like you that will destroy mankind's only chance to live in peace and happiness," Major Frank told her.

He knocked on the door of Mica's shipboard office.

"Come in," Mica replied.

Major Frank tossed the woman into the room and pushed her down into a chair opposite Mica. He stood over her, the gun still at her temple.

"You're a big disappointment to me, Coco," Link said. "You could have been with me to enjoy the fruits of my labors."

Coco glared at him. "What do you mean, Link?"

Mica ignored her. "The Major tells me that you are working for the KGB. Well, that evens things out. We had a couple of agents before you from the CIA. I must congratulate you, though. You were the first one to fully gain my confidence."

"What are you going to do with me?" she asked him.

"I won't kill you, if that's what you're thinking. I'm just going to reprogram you by exposing you to correct thoughts."

"What are correct thoughts?"

"Universally correct thoughts. Peace, love, friendship, honor—those thoughts are correct for all men everywhere. I will see to it that the world is exposed to the things that will bring this planet true happiness."

"You're crazy!" Coco told him.

Major Frank slapped her hard across the face. "You show some respect," he told her.

"I expect to be called crazy. Christ was called crazy. Moses, Buddha, they were all thought to be crazy because they dared to follow a different path. They all strove to unify the world under one banner, but they were doomed to failure because the technology wasn't perfected in their time. I will succeed. The world has shrunk to manageable size, due to satellites, computers, and communication advances. Science is now a religion, and I am its High Priest and World Savior."

"I don't understand you, Link," she said, looking at him and shaking her head in disbelief.

"You will. You will be exposed to the correct thoughts and then you will know everything. You can take her away, Major."

Major Frank lifted her from her chair and pushed her out the door. He dragged her to the top deck, up the landing pad, and pushed her through the glass doors of the chopper.

The pilot, another one of Mica's Security people, paid her no attention at all.

"Let's get moving," Major Frank commanded.

The pilot pressed the starter, and the chopper rose off the ship.

"Where are you taking me?" she wanted to know.

"You wanted to see The Facility on Mica Island. Now your wish is going to come true."

Dr. Townsend sat next to Karen in the air-conditioned, glass-enclosed cafeteria. She was going over the written reports of two of the counselors Dr. Townsend had asked her to supervise. In addition, Karen herself had a caseload of three patients. One of her patients was the Minister of Education in Sweden, Gunther Glass.

"Good morning, Karen. How are you today?"

She looked up at him and gave Dr. Townsend a brilliant smile. "Robert, hi. Isn't it a lovely morning?"

He didn't answer her, so she said it again. He probably had forgotten to turn up the volume on his hearing aid. "Lovely morning!" she yelled.

"Oh, yes. Just beautiful. Just a minute while I fiddle with this." He adjusted the tiny wheel behind his ear. "How's Gunther doing?"

"It's just amazing. He's had a regular sleep pattern for two nights now. If he's accurate in what he says, that's the first time he's been able to get more than one hour's rest in ten years."

"Another small miracle," Townsend said ruefully.

"It's just phenomenal what progress is being made here," Karen said exuberantly.

"Now if we can only find out how we do it," Townsend said.

"It doesn't really matter as long as it works, Robert."

"Well, it's important to—"

"I think the major importance is to cure the patient. That's what we're here for. I'm very pleased that people are getting well, so they can go back to their own lands and bring the message to others."

Townsend looked at her and scratched his cheek. "And what would that message be?"

"That the world has to unite to stop war and hatred. That we all must live as brothers with respect and love."

Townsend nodded. "I see. Just a few days ago,

110

Karen, you were disturbed at the rate of cures we were achieving. Now that doesn't seem to bother you."

"Robert, it's our job to help these people as much and as quickly as possible. We can't spare any energy to make sure the guests are well. They are the future. They're the ones who will lead mankind down a path of happiness and prosperity. The quicker we can help the guests over their addiction, the more people we can work with."

"Why do you think we are so successful, Karen?"

"Because we represent an idea, a force. The guests know they have a mission. They *want* to get well. They *want* to carry out their roles to help Link."

"Help Link? What do you mean, 'Help Link,' my dear?"

"Robert, I can't explain now. It's just so wonderful to be a part of all this. I really have to go now. I want to look in on Gunther, and I have a staff meeting in a quarter of an hour. Thank you, Robert, for asking me to join you."

"Not at all. It's wonderful having you and your enthusiasm here at The Facility," Townsend said.

He watched as she bounded out of the cafeteria, down the flowered walk toward the Psychology Staff Building. Something she said kept repeating in his head.

They want to carry out their roles to help Link.

It reminded him of something. He had read

literature of the Stalin era in Russia, and the Mao era in China. Those two men had fostered a so-called "cult of personality" in which every achievement, every success, could be attributed to the leader's beneficence or wisdom. Personal failures became a direct betrayal of the leader.

Now that Karen mentioned it, he realized that the patients, or guests as Link called them, always left The Facility praising the wonderful Link Mica. People working on The Facility tried to do a good job in the hope that they would be reported to Link Mica. If someone did a job poorly, the idea that Link might be told sent them into a cold sweat.

But how does one instill a cult of personality when no indoctrination is taking place, he wondered. For that matter, how does one cure lifelong addictions by using traditional methodology that has always had only marginal success at best?

He had been putting it off as long as possible. Now it was time to get some answers.

In three days, Karen Aztec's inquisitive and brilliant mind had been reduced to platitudes. He had brought her here. He was responsible for what happened to her.

Link Mica had used him as a shill in a con game. He couldn't wait any longer. He had to see Link and get some answers.

Ben Kane took a booth in the downtown soda

fountain spot known as the Crazy Cow. A couple of cruise ships had landed at Charlotte Amalie in St. Thomas and the streets were crowded with tourists from Japan, Germany, and the States.

Within minutes, the stores along Dronningens Gade would be filled to capacity, doing goldrush business, buoyed by the trumpeting of the tourist boards and publicity agents that St. Thomas is a duty-free port.

Ben checked his watch and surveyed the room once again. Ganja had agreed to the job and had gotten an interview scheduled with Mrs. Baxter of The Facility. Weaver had given him a new identity as Nick Garrett. His papers said he had been in the Marines and seen duty in Nam. He was also listed as an expert in all kinds of weaponry. That at least wasn't made up. Ganja was one of those natural-born marksmen who was as proficient with a handgun as he was with a cannon. In addition, growing up on the streets of Harlem had given him some essential training in using a knife.

Ben had reasoned, and Ganja agreed, that based on what had happened in Pelican Cove, the Mica people would definitely need replacement security people.

Ganja walked into the Crazy Cow and walked directly to a table at the far end of the restaurant. He didn't turn to see if Kane was there. He took a seat with his back to the door. That was standard operating procedure. It was now Ben's job to keep an eye on the door to see if Ganja had picked up a tail along the way.

Ganja looked clear. No one followed him in. After a few minutes, Ben got up and joined the Ganja man.

"How did it go, Nick?" Kane asked him, using the alias.

"Perfect. When I talked about my military background, her eyes lit up. She told me they had some spots that could be filled in Security."

"I'll bet."

"She gave me a contract to sign. It was the standard three-month deal."

"Any surprises? Anything out of the ordinary?"

Ganja shrugged. "Not really. Except the way this Mrs. Baxter talked about Link Mica. Her voice sort of lowered when she mentioned his name, like she was talking about some kind of god. Her office was decorated with pictures of the dude on every wall."

"He's got, as they say in the supermarket tabloids, charisma."

"If I were worth a billion bucks, you can be sure I'd get me a little of that charisma stuff myself," Ganja said.

"When do you start?" Kane asked him.

"First thing tomorrow morning. A chopper takes me out to the island, and I meet a Major Frank in the Security Building."

"Good. I don't want you staying on that island one second longer than you have to. Try to find out what's going on and then get the hell out."

"Aye, aye, Skip."

"Weaver sent you a present. It's the latest gizmo thought up by the whizzes at Ultratech."

Kane handed Ganja a small jewelry box. He opened it and picked up the large crucifix with Christ's eyes in diamonds.

"You mean he's going to miss me after all," Ganja said jokingly.

"Let me show you how it works," Kane told him. "What you have there is a sophisticated tracking device. It sends out a beam of energy every fifteen seconds. As long as you wear it, we'll be able to track your whereabouts on the island. If you find that you need help, what you do is press the left eye once and hold it for five seconds, then press the right eye and hold it for five seconds. That will change the pulse from once every fifteen seconds to every five seconds."

"Okay, if I get into trouble, I call on Jesus."

"Chief and I will be just out of the territorial limits of the island. You get to the beach, and we'll pick you up."

"Okay, Skip," Ganja agreed. "Sharon gave me a picture of Jacob, so I know who I'm looking for."

"Even more important than Jacob is Mica's ability to brainwash. Just make sure you don't become a convert."

"Can you see me in that army marching belly first into a machine-gun nest? No way."

CHAPTER 12

Link Mica had his helicopter pilot circle once around The Facility before they touched down. There were seven buildings in the compound, each shining white, two stories high. The chopper landed on the roof of the Administration Building, and Link walked down the short flight of stairs to his office.

The office was sparsely furnished, with a desk, a chair and couch, and a file cabinet. Behind the chair, taking up a good part of the wall, was the Mica insignia.

There were several reports on the desk, and Link

read through them quickly, using the skills he'd developed at speed reading.

There was a light tap at the door and Mrs. Baxter stepped in. "Hello, Link," she said nervously.

"Lynne, how are you?" He rose out of his chair and gave her a peck on the cheek.

She flushed and smiled at him. "I just wanted to let you know that I took care of that Peters thing. I don't want you to be concerned."

Link nodded. "It happens, Lynne. Don't blame yourself. There's got to be some that slip through the cracks."

"If they were only bright enough to understand what we're doing. Why do they make it so difficult?"

"Have patience, Lynne. You can't change the world in a week or two. You've got to give me at least a year," he said, winking.

"Oh, Link," she sighed deeply. "I just thank God a man like you can come along with the vision to save us."

"It's not just me, Lynne. It's all of us. We're a team. We've got a mission, and together we can see it through. If Link Mica disappeared tomorrow, it would be up to you and the others to carry on what we've started here."

Lynne's eyes clouded over. "Please, Link. Don't say such a thing. I couldn't bear the thought of you—"

"Now come on, Lynne. I'm not going anywhere. There's too much still to be done. By the way, did you notice if Dr. Townsend was waiting to see me?"

"Yes, he was outside when I came in."

"Do me a favor and send him in. And Lynne, keep up the good work."

"Sure, Link," she said. She smiled and backed out the door.

Townsend knocked and walked into the office. Link walked over and shook hands with him. He sat down with the doctor on the couch and clasped his hands with his index fingers, touching his lips in thoughtful repose.

"Robert, you said you had something urgent to talk to me about. I hope you're feeling well. It's not that gall bladder thing again, is it?"

"No, Link, nothing like that."

"Can I get you something, Robert? A cup of coffee, or that tea you're so fond of?"

"No, thank you. You're very kind."

"How about something with a little more kick? I think you like scotch, right?"

"Yes, I do, Link. Your memory for detail is astounding, as usual, but I think you'd better hear what I have to say."

Link shrugged. "Sounds very serious. Go ahead, Robert."

The older man slipped on a pair of wire-rimmed glasses and took a folded piece of yellow legal paper out of his pocket.

"Link, I've had over one hundred and sixty cases to date in The Facility. Some of these people

had addictions that had lasted their entire lives.
The median amount of years for their afflictions
was eighteen. One hundred and fifty-seven of
those people stayed on the island over one week.
We were able to effect a cure for every single one
of them," Townsend said, peering over his glasses.

"That's sensational!" Mica said, beaming.

"No, Link, it's a miracle. I'm a psychologist,
not a miracle worker."

"I don't follow you. Aren't you happy with those
results?"

"I'm delighted with the results. I just don't
understand how they're possible."

"But, Robert, I thought we had already dis-
cussed this matter. I thought we agreed that the
amazing success we've been having has to do with
dedicated staff members and the idyllic surroundings, which foster a climate of health and well-
being."

"Yes, Link, I know we talked about that."

Townsend took off his glasses, folded them
slowly, and placed them back in his shirt pocket.
"I suppose I was looking for some kind of explanation. I must admit I got carried away, flushed with
success." His voice trailed off.

"So, Robert, how do we account for those
numbers?" Link asked, his eyes narrowing.

"I think you know that better than I do, Link.
You know how much I admire you. There's no
question in my mind that you are one of the
brightest men that ever lived. But somehow you've

devised a method to do the impossible. I don't know why you want to continue the charade so people think it has something to do with me or my staff."

"Well, I'm flattered, Robert. Quite frankly, when The Facility was just starting, it was important to have a man of your stature involved with it. Now, though, our operation has achieved the recognition we need and your help isn't all that vital. As a matter of fact, I've been reading some reports, and I'm quite impressed with Miss Aztec."

"What have you done to her, Link?"

"In order for my plan to succeed, I need unquestioning dedication. Let's just say that I made certain of that dedication."

"Link," Townsend said, running his hand through his steel-gray hair, "you must have reasons for all this. You've somehow enslaved all of these people, and I'd like to know why."

"Not for any personal gain, Robert. I have a mission that I'm destined to fulfill."

"Tell me about it," Townsend said.

Link laughed. "Do you think you can psychoanalyze me, Robert? Do you think you'll be able to talk me out of my delusions?"

"I'm just trying to understand, Link."

"You can't understand, at least not fully. You're an intelligent man, Robert, so I'll try to explain some things to you. I don't expect you to approve of what I say. Because of your training, my behavior will seem deviant, yet I am convinced that I am correct, and nothing is going to stop me."

"I want to understand, Link," Townsend told him in a soothing voice.

"Well, to get on with it, after reviewing the facts, I became convinced that mankind would destroy itself within three years—five, at most. More and more countries are stockpiling nuclear weapons. Certain germ warfare experiments being carried on around the world will make the H-bomb seem like a blessing from God. Add to this scenario of world destruction, the satellite laser technology that can beam down a ray of heat and decimate continents."

"But Link, there are people trying to limit arms build-up. The United Nations—"

"Too little and too late, my friend. I can see the sand in the hourglass, and time is running out. There is only one answer, and that is world domination by one man. One man who controls the means of production, one man who controls all governments, one man who controls all armies. One man who can solve the problems of hunger and pestilence and war."

"And that man is you," Townsend said quietly.

"Robert, it's my destiny. I'm really not an egomaniac. I have all the power I need, I have all the money I need. I'm doing this for mankind. I believe I was put on this earth in order to save it."

"I see," Townsend said.

"No, you don't. You can't see. You're limited by your training and your intellect. You hear what I say, but your mind is thinking that this man is crazy. I know; you can't help yourself."

"Even if what you say is possible, how is curing addicts or brainwashing the island staff into absolute fidelity going to enable you to conquer the world?"

"You are seeing just tiny pieces of the larger picture, my friend. Those people who have come to The Facility to be cured are walking away with much more. They are the leaders, the power brokers, the trend setters. And they have been reprogrammed."

Link stood up and walked behind his desk. "Robert, you called the cures of the one hundred and fifty-seven people miracles. I have achieved something that two hundred years of scientific thought couldn't come close to doing. I can control people's brains and make them do what I program them to do. You've seen this at The Facility on a small scale. Now picture it worldwide."

"How do you do it, Link?"

"Through the headphones. I found that by adding frequencies of certain pitch and duration, various parts of the cerebellum and cortex could be stimulated. By stimulating the brain, using the correct code of pitch and duration, people could be programmed. An infinite amount of signals can be sent over the airwaves. For people in the Staff Building, I made them the best loyal workers possible. For people in the Security wing, I programmed them to be fearless unthinking soldiers.

It was child's play to cure the guests and make them forever grateful to me. Each was given a special task to perform upon leaving The Facility."

"You're bluffing. It's simply not possible!"

"You know it is true, Robert. It's very disturbing to you, isn't it?"

"Link, I've spent my whole life trying to free the mind from imprisonment. You've just substituted one type of nightmare for another."

"I knew you would see it that way. It's a shame, because I was hoping you might want to help me develop this further."

"Why? You seem to have all the answers."

"Not quite. It seems that after six months, the body seems to form some kind of defense mechanism and—"

"Damn! You're getting a rebound effect. They could go insane."

"Yes. Insane or suicidal."

"Link, you've got to stop this. I beg you."

"Don't be silly. We haven't even started."

Townsend shook his head. "It won't work, Link. There are people out there that won't be susceptible. I slept with the phones on; it had no effect on me."

Link nodded. "I wondered about that. I started to believe that perhaps people of superior intellect could resist. I've already found that if correct thoughts are forced upon someone and they know it's coming, it's much more difficult to reprogram them. I'm trying some experiments, as we speak, on some of my enemies. Although it's difficult, everyone eventually receives the correct thoughts.

"There's a very simple explanation why you haven't been reprogrammed and it has more to do with your physical makeup than your mental prowess. Your hearing affliction made it impossible for you to pick up the tone variations. That's why you weren't affected. I don't mind, really. You weren't hurting anything, so I felt I'd just leave you alone."

"Now what, Link? Now do I get reprogrammed, too?"

"No, there's no need to. I told you before we don't have any use for you."

"You mean you'll just let me out of here? You'll let me go back to my work?"

Then Robert's eyes opened, and very softly, he said, "no."

Link had reached into the drawer of his desk and pulled out a nickel-plated revolver.

The gun coughed twice. The first bullet pierced the old man's heart, smashing the glasses in his breast pocket. The other bullet entered the side of his head, splintering the bones of his skull.

He was dead before he hit the ground.

CHAPTER 13

Ben walked aboard the *Wu Li* and knew immediately that someone had been on board his boat. He had his own warning system, a piece of Scotch tape on the top corner between the door and the jamb. If the tape was split, that meant someone had opened the door and gone below deck.

He reached into his pocket and wrapped his hand around the deadly .22 Beretta. The two other guns Ben used, the Smith and Wesson .357 magnum and the French MAB 9mm automatic, were locked away in his cabin.

The cartridge in the chamber and the first one in

the clip were regular cartridges, which Kane fired as warning shots. The others in the clip were high-speed hollow point .22LR cartridges, which expanded on contact and could bring down anything smaller than a Buick.

Kane took off his shoes and walked slowly across the deck, avoiding the spots that might creak and alert anyone down below. He heard sounds of somebody moving in the galley. There was no way to go below deck without exposing himself to a line of fire. He decided to take the chance that whoever was down there would be taken by surprise. Whoever it was wasn't taking any pains to be quiet.

Kane dived down the narrow staircase, the Beretta pointed in front of him. He hit the bottom and rolled to the side, and ended up in front of a pair of legs in jeans.

The legs belonged to Jessica Carlisle.

"If you use the stairs, you'll find it's less wear and tear on your clothes," she said.

Ben stood up sheepishly. "What are you doing on my boat?" he asked her, quickly putting the gun back in his pocket.

"I wanted to see you. I knew Karen wasn't here, so I wouldn't embarrass you. And your other little playmate, Michelle, is off in the States. So, I thought it might be a good time to stake my claim."

"Stake your claim?"

"That's an American expression, isn't it? What I mean, Ben, is that I've decided that you're worth fighting for. I am willing to put up a battle for you. I shan't play upper crust and leave the field open to my competition."

"Well, I—"

"I've made you some coffee and I brought over some home-baked pie. I'm sure it will taste horribly, but I want some points for trying."

"I thought I locked the door."

"You did. You also gave me a key and told me I may come aboard anytime I cared to."

"I remember that. You said, 'Don't hold your breath.'"

"Well, I'm not playing hard to get anymore. The fact is, you know I'm fond of you. Well, more than fond of you. I also know you care about me. Oh, posh. Have a slice of pie."

He pulled her close to him and kissed her passionately on the lips. He felt her respond to him, her body pressing against his, her need causing her breath to come in sharp little gulps of air.

"I think you missed me," he told her, breaking away for a moment.

He took her into his stateroom, and she was all over him. He started to get undressed, but she wouldn't let him.

"I'll do it, she whispered. "You just relax."

When he was completely nude, it was her turn. She stood up and slowly took off her blouse and pants. She stood close to the bed, just out of reach, in her yellow bikini panties and matching bra. He tried to grab her, but she just moved farther out of his reach.

"I see you want me," she said, looking down at his rock-hard erection.

She undid the clasps of her bra and let her milky white breasts spill forward.

"Get over here!" he ordered.

"Not yet."

She turned her back on him and sensuously lowered the briefs down the silky columns of her buttocks. When she turned around, she stood before him, legs slightly apart. She was all woman, with rose-tipped nipples, an hourglass waist, and soft, rounded hips surrounding the honey-blond mound of her sex.

One of her hands reached up to cup her breast. Her fingers tweaked and rolled her nipples as her hot eyes watched him and her tongue flicked at the corners of her mouth. Her other hand snaked down slowly between her legs. She spread herself wider.

"Jessica," Ben breathed.

He couldn't take a second more of her teasing. He reached out and brought her down on the bed, crushing her back against his chest. He entered her quickly.

She closed her eyes and leaned back, feeling him probe the depths of her hot core as she began to move. "Ben," she whispered.

He teased her, used her, brought her right to the brink and then held back, feeling her passion and frustration.

"Damn you," she said, her movements becoming desperate. Rising to her knees, she drew Kane up. He began to pound her eagerly from behind.

He felt her strong inner muscles grabbing him, kneading him. They both began to moan as their orgasms grew closer. Finally, they exploded together, their bodies moving frantically in the cabin's dim light.

CHAPTER 14

Ganja was standing with two other new recruits. One man's name was Steve, the other was George. Major Frank stood next to them, his eyes on his troops. They were on a parade field, in full uniform under the blistering Caribbean sun.

"You are about to become part of the most dedicated fighting force the world has ever known," the Major told them. "Each of these men is a fighting machine capable of taking down seventy enemies. We are fearless, we are courageous, we are willing to die to defend what we believe in. Are you men ready to take your place among us?"

"Yes, sir!" Ganja and the two others said.

"I don't hear you."

"Yes, sir!"

"I still don't hear you."

"YES, SIR!" they screamed at the top of their lungs.

"Which one of you men is Nick Garrett?" Frank asked.

"I'm Nick," Ganja said.

"You're the arms expert, huh. You think of yourself as a marksman, do you?"

"I've been told I'm pretty good, sir."

Frank pulled a rifle from one of the men standing close to them. He tossed it at Ganja.

"Let's see what you can do, Garrett. Take a look at that rock near the Security Building. Do you see the bottle on the rock?"

"Yes, sir."

"Can you hit it?"

It was a difficult shot only because Ganja didn't know if the rifle sight on the M16 was accurate. If he had a chance to fire the gun a few times . . .

"I asked if you could hit it, son."

"I think I can."

"We don't use words like *think*, or *maybe*, or *perhaps*."

"I can hit it, sir," Ganja told him.

"Then do it.!"

He aimed the gun and squeezed the trigger slowly. The bottle exploded. The faintest tinkling sound coming back to them.

"That was good shooting," Major Frank grudgingly admitted.

"Unfortunately, you don't usually shoot at bottles in a war," a voice behind them said.

Ganja turned around. It was the man in all of Mrs. Baxter's pictures, Link Mica.

"At-ten-shun!!" Major Frank yelled, and the soldiers clicked into place as precisely as gears on a Swiss timepiece.

"Put them at ease, Major," Link said.

He was wearing shorts, a T-shirt, and sneakers without socks.

"What's your name?" he asked Ganja.

"Nick Garrett," Ganja told him.

"How do you do under pressure, Nick?"

"The best I can."

Mica thought about that answer. The man next to Ganja, George, had a pack of cigarettes in his pocket. Mica reached over and withdrew the pack. He took out one cigarette and stared at Ganja. He broke the cigarette in half.

"I'd like to see some volunteers who'd be willing to walk down to the rock over there and stick this half cigarette in his mouth and have Garrett here shoot it out. Can I see some hands of volunteers?"

Nick couldn't believe his eyes. Every single man, including Major Frank, raised his hand. Only Steve, George, and Ganja had their hands down.

Mica looked at the three new men and smiled. "You pick one," he said to Ganja.

135

"It's dangerous. I could kill someone."

"There's no such thing as a noble death, my friend. Getting killed proving a point to me is as important as any other way of dying. Now, choose someone," Mica ordered.

Ganja looked at the men with their hands raised. One looked as good as another, so he chose the man whose rifle he had been given. The man stepped out of line and walked up to Mica without batting an eye. Mica handed him the cigarette and the man walked down to the same rock where Ganja had hit the bottle. The man stuck the cigarette in his lips and turned, to present Ganja with his profile.

Ganja took a long sigh. He lifted the gun, and then brought it down as a bead of sweat dropped into his eye from his forehead. He wiped his eye with his hand and raised the rifle again.

"Go ahead," Mica told him. "Pull the trigger!"

The gun recoiled and the cigarette went flying out of the man's lips. He picked it up and brought it over to Mica for his inspection. If he was scared—or relieved, for that matter—you couldn't tell.

"Excellent, Mr. Garrett. Excellent!" Mica beamed. "You're quite a good shot. Now how about some turnabout, as they say. What goes around, comes around. Which of you three gentlemen would like to try it with another half cigarette and let one of my soldiers shoot it out of your mouth?" Link asked.

"Uh, no thanks," Steve mumbled, turning pale.

"I'd um, rather not," George begged off.

"What about you, Garrett? You seem to be a man with iron nerves."

"I'd rather depend on myself, Mr. Mica, sir."

Mica nodded. "Not a bad answer. One thing you'll learn here, though, is that the individual counts for very little. It's the entire group that takes precedence. I want to assure all of you new recruits that in a short period of time, you will have the iron nerves and the fortitude to be proud additions to the Mica family. You'll find that, like these men, you'll be ready for anything.

"Very good, Major Frank. Carry on, men."

Ganja joined Steve and George at a table in the cafeteria of the Security Building. Like the other buildings in The Facility, this one was a sprawling white edifice two stories high. The second story contained most of the living quarters, generally three men to a room. The ground floor housed the huge cafeteria and the offices of Major Frank and his personal staff. The security people ate in their own cafeteria while the guests and the staff ate in the restaurant-style facility in the Guests Building.

George and Steve had built up an appetite after Major Frank had put them through a series of calisthenics with the regular forces. Ganja had thought he was in pretty good shape, but he found he'd have to work hard to maintain the level of fitness that the Mica people had achieved.

They were a scary bunch, he decided. He had never seen a group of men so totally dedicated to what they were doing. They followed every order from Major Frank and seemed to relish putting their bodies through rigorous physical torture. Every command was carried out at top speed, and there was never a groan or a muttering under the breath.

The fact was, there was no conversation at all. Each of the guards of soldiers looked like they were cut from the same cookie cutter. The regulation haircut—Ganja and the other new men would get theirs tomorrow—and the uniforms made each of them the same as the next man. There were brown skins, white skins, and black skins, but in the green uniform of the Mica army, they all appeared to be interchangeable parts.

"Hey, Nick," Steve whispered. "These guys are weirdos, right?"

"They're different, all right," Ganja admitted.

"I was in the Green Berets, and I thought I knew about tough outfits. But, shit!"

"What's with these guys? Look at them eating. Nobody talks to one another. It's like eating in a church around here," George said.

"I spoke to one of them," Steve said. "I asked him if it was always so quiet around the barracks. I tried to make a joke out of it."

"Did he answer you?" George wanted to know.

"Maybe it's some kind of dumb initiation thing. Nobody talks to the new guys."

"I asked him if the guys had all taken a vow of silence, like monks," Steve continued. "You know what he says to me?"

"I don't know if I want to know," George said.

"The guy looks up from his push-ups and says that talk is a waste of time. He says we've got to keep thinking of how to be a better soldier and how to best serve the unit."

"Shit!" Ganja replied.

"I hate that Regular Army bull. I can't believe these guys are serious," Steve said.

"Man, they're serious! Did you see them all raise their hands when Mica wanted a volunteer for Nick's target practice?"

The two men shook their heads and continued to eat their food. They had been given what looked to be an excellent steak, vegetables and fruits, and juices. There certainly seemed to be a lot of food, and no one was shy about going back to the long buffet tables for seconds or thirds.

"At least the grub is delicious," George said. "What's wrong, Nick? You haven't touched anything."

Ganja eyed the food with suspicion. Something was turning these Security guys into zombies; maybe it was the food.

"Too much workout this afternoon. My stomach's not ready."

"Yeah. I thought I could take it, but brother."

Steve shook his head.

Ganja had promised Kane and Sharon that he'd try to get to the bottom of what was going on at The Facility and get out of there as fast as possible. He was wasting time. Jacob Peters was probably serving food in the guest restaurant.

"Hey, look, you guys. I've got to check out the head. Cover for me in case anybody wants to know where I am" Ganja told them.

"You got it, Nick," Steve said. "The three of us better stick together."

They had given Ganja a mini-tour when he arrived so he had a basic idea in his mind where everything was. The Guest Building was just off the center of the island. Next to it were the Senior Staff cottages. The Senior Staff people were the only people on the island that didn't live in a dormitory-style set-up. Ganja had been told that the guests had their own private rooms, but those rooms weren't much different than the rooms in the Security Building or the Food Services Building.

It was a cloudy, moonless night, and Ganja felt at home among the tall brush and mild sea breezes. He stayed off the floral paths and the tiled walks, choosing instead to circle the long way around in order to avoid anyone else who wasn't in the buildings.

He was wearing a green Mica T-shirt and green-and-red shorts. He was told that he would be issued a uniform like the rest of the security people within a week. What he was wearing suited Ganja just fine. It was the standard outfit of the men and women who serviced the guests. If by chance someone did see him, he fit right in with most of the people on The Facility.

He came to the Guest Building and looked through the large ground-floor windows at the people inside the restaurant. There were three tables, with up to twenty-five guests at each.

Ganja looked over the smiling, animated faces. The guests at least seemed to be having a good time. It was some contrast to the Security mess hall. The restaurant was painted in powder blue and bright yellow shades. There were pictures of food and paintings with food themes on the walls.

The guests were served by native Virgin Islanders, who seemed to be working hard but also seemed to be enjoying waiting on the guests.

Ganja looked over the guests. These were supposed to be the richest and most powerful people of the world. Two-thirds of them were men, and the third who were women were mostly older than the men. Ganja thought he recognized a face or two belonging to people who might have chartered a yacht from Caribbean Dream, then he thought better of it. These people didn't have to charter. They all had their own yachts.

Jacob Peters didn't seem to be out front in the restaurant. Chances were he was working as a chef and was still in the kitchen. Ganja moved toward the back of the building, making sure to use the trees that surrounded the place as cover. He came to the back and noticed a large garbage bin. Where there was a garbage bin, there was a door to bring out the garbage, and near that door would be the kitchen.

Just as he figured out where he'd have to go, the door opened and a black man wearing a blood-stained white apron walked out to the back. He was well over six feet tall and weighed about two-fifty. He had thick hands, and with the stains on the apron, Ganja guessed he was a butcher. The man took out a cigarette, leaned against the bin, and lit it up.

Ganja stepped out from behind the tree and walked over to him. "Hey, mon, how's it goin'," Ganja said, using the West Indian patois he had mastered during his stay on the Virgins.

The man nodded. "No complaints," he said.

"Is Jacob inside?" Ganja asked, tilting his head toward the door, which he presumed led to the kitchen.

"What you want Jacob for, mon?" It was more conversational than curious.

"He los' somting and they want me to fetch him so he can pick it up."

"I give it to him. I'm Little John, his next-door roommate."

"Sorry, mon. I got to fetch him meself. You know how they are when they give you a task. They got to make sure it is done exactly right."

"Nobody gives me a problem," Little John said, surprised that Ganja seemed to be having trouble.

"No, mon. No problem on The Facility. It's within me to do things the way I tink they should be done."

Little John nodded his agreement. "That's it, mon. You do things right for the good of everybody."

Ganja nodded.

"No, he went bock to the building, room 245. I tink he not been well lately."

"Okay, Little John. I'll look him up there." Ganja smiled and walked away, leaving Little John to his smoke.

The Food Services Building looked the same as the others. There was a sign on the marble front that said FOOD SERVICES. One of the Security guards was standing under the sign, his M16 on his shoulder.

Ganja wondered if he could walk right by him as if he were someone who lived in the building, or should he carry on with the story he had told Little John about having to take Peters to the Administration Building to pick up some lost property. Then he rejected those ideas. The guard was probably one of the men who was on the parade grounds that afternoon. He had probably gotten a good look at Ganja then.

Instead, Ganja picked up a rock and threw it at the glass window on the far side of the building entrance. He counted on the guard being super-diligent, willing to check out every noise. He was right. The Mica Security man crouched low and eased his gun off his shoulder. He stared around for a moment, looking like a dog trying to pick up a scent. Then he walked away from the front, toward the area where Ganja had thrown the rock.

Ganja had only a couple of seconds, so he moved fast. He slipped into the building and up the stairs before the guard turned around.

He walked down the thick-carpeted hallway until he came to a room 245. He knocked lightly on the door, but got no answer. He knocked louder; still no answer.

Then he heard a man moan loudly.

Ganja turned the door knob and looked in. There was a man on one of the beds. He had an icepack on his head and both hands pressed against his temples. He moaned again.

"Are you all right?" Ganja asked, walking over to the bed.

"Who are you?" the man asked, looking up and trying to focus his eyes.

Ganja recognized him. It was Jacob Peters.

"I'm a friend," Ganja said. "Can I do anything for you?"

The man fell back on his pillow. "Ohh, it hurts so much. Nothing helps. Not ice, aspirin. Ohh, my head hurts bad."

"I'll call a doctor for you."

The man didn't move. Ganja thought he hadn't

heard him.

"The doctor can't help. I been to the doctor, and they can't help. I just have to wait until it passes."

"How long does it take to pass?"

"Soon . . . It will be over soon."

Jacob seemed to know what he was talking about. It was obvious he couldn't respond to any of Ganja's questions while he was in such a painful state. Ganja waited, hoping Peters would pull out of it.

Eventually, Peters wiped his face with his hands and sat up. "That was a bad one," he said, shaking his head as if to clear the cobwebs.

"How long have you had these headaches?" Ganja asked him.

"They started recently, and they've been coming more and more frequently. Hey, who are you, man?"

"I told you before, I'm a friend."

"I don't know your face."

"I know yours, Jacob. Your girlfriend showed me your picture."

"Girlfriend? What do you mean, 'girlfriend'?"

Ganja looked at him. He sincerely didn't seem to know what Ganja was talking about. "Sharon," Ganja said.

"I don't know any Sharon," he replied.

"You are Jacob Peters, right?"

"Yes."

Ganja wondered if the headaches had something to do with him losing his memory.

"Where are you from, Jacob?"

"I'm from here, the Food Services Building."

"And before that?"

"I'm from here, Jacob insisted. "I don't know any Sharon, and I don't know who you are."

"You were supposed to marry Sharon. You had come on the island to get money for a house. Don't you remember anything?"

"No."

"Tell me about your headaches. You didn't have any headache when you gave that man a note to give to Sharon."

"I don't remember," Peters said. "Please leave me alone. I've got to go back to work. It doesn't matter how one man feels, it's the job of the one to work for the many."

Ganja nodded. There was nothing left to say.

Ganja left him and stepped out into the hall. He made his way to the stairs and looked out front for the guard. He was still standing there, his rifle slung once again over his shoulder.

Ganja walked briskly out the door and, after he passed the guard, whistled nonchalantly. He waited for the guard to tell him to stop, or to follow him, but it didn't happen.

Now he walked down the tile paths until he got to the Security Building. He walked inside; three-quarters of the soldiers were gone. George and Steve weren't at the table.

He turned and walked toward the staircase. He knew he and the other two had been assigned to room 206.

Major Frank was waiting for him on the second floor. "Where've you been, Garrett?"

"Bad stomach, sir," Ganja said.

"I checked the bathrooms and you weren't there."

"I know."

"What does that mean?"

"I know I wasn't in the bathroom, sir."

Major Frank's eyes narrowed. "I don't want any damn doubletalk from you, Garrett. I want to know where the hell you've been for the past forty minutes."

Ganja's mind raced. "It's kind of personal, sir."

"Spill it!"

"Well, Major, I've got a nervous stomach. I saw the kind of men in the outfit and I was nervous that I wouldn't shape up. I started getting the heaves, sir. I went into the head in the Security Building, and then I realized that some of the men might be coming in. I didn't want them to see me heaving my guts up like that, so I went out to find another head in another building. I think it was the Administration Building, sir. I used the head there, sir."

Major Frank was thinking it over. It looked like he bought it.

"I don't want you to be nervous, Garrett. All the men start out wondering if they can shape up. That's natural. From now on, you talk to me if you've got to leave the group. You pull a stunt like that again and you'll really have something to be nervous about! Do you understand?"

"Yes, sir!"

Major Frank started to walk away, then he turned. "I thought you said you were in the Marine Corps on Nam."

"Yes, sir."

"How come you call a bathroom a 'head'? That's a Navy term, isn't it?"

"Yes, sir. After the Marines, I worked for fishing outfits. I guess some of the lingo stuck."

"We've got a lot of boats on patrol around the island. Maybe you'd like duty like that?"

"Anything, sir, to serve the many."

"Yeah, well, that might be something to look into. Good night, Garrett, and don't forget what I said. And don't forget to put on your headphones tonight."

"Sir?"

"By your bed you'll find a set of headphones. Wear them to sleep. They'll help you get a restful sleep and give you an edge to cope with tomorrow. You might find it's so soothing that it cures that stomach of yours."

"Yes, sir. I'll wear the headphones," Ganja told him.

He made his way to the room. He wasn't surprised to see the room was exactly like Jacob Peters'.

Steve and George were in their beds, asleep already. They each had on a set of black headphones.

Ganja walked over to the remaining bed and sat down on it. The mattress was firm and comfortable. The linens were spotlessly clean and smelled fresh.

He lifted up the headphones and put them on. The sound was very pleasant, like the sound of the surf breaking against the rocks. Ganja could see how the headphones could put someone to sleep. In just a few seconds he was feeling drowsy.

There was a sign in the room that caught Ganja's eye:

ALL PERSONNEL MUST WEAR
HEADPHONES BEFORE GOING TO SLEEP.

Ganja became wary. Ben had warned him to be careful of anything out of the ordinary.

Tonight he'd pass on the headphones.

CHAPTER 15

Chief Bukowski was waiting for Ben on board the specially armed, deep V-hulled Leopard 19. The Leopard, using GM 12-71 turbos, could do better than 25 knots. It was an excellent, fast-cruising yacht and Ben, Miles, and Bukowski could be comfortable on board in the stateroom and guest berths.

Another reason the Chief settled on the Leopard when he chose a boat for the mission was that the slick, powerful yacht could also easily carry the Sanger Alley Cat. That gave them some firepower, with the Leopard's two 7.62mm cannons and twin

20mm Gatling guns, and speed, with the Alley Cat ready to pounce at over a hundred miles an hour.

Miles was already on board. The gaunt ex-SEAL wore a pair of faded denim shorts, without a shirt. His wiry, bronzed body bore the scars and burns of dangerous assignments. He was tying a knot in the line, untying it, and tying it again.

Ben walked along the deck and inspected the boat.

"How does she feel, Chief?" Kane asked.

"Ready to roll, Commander."

"Okay, then. Let's take her out."

Bukowski navigated the channel and took the boat into the open water. Kane stood on the flying bridge and stared out at the ocean water.

"Something troubling you, Ben?" Bukowski asked him.

"No. Well, yeah. Something Jessica told me." Kane jammed his hands in his jeans and shook his head. "It seems her Uncle Reggie left their place the other night, went back to his hotel, and, without a word of warning, blew out his brains with a shotgun."

"Jesus, Ben! Weren't you there talking to the man?"

"It happened the next night."

"That must have been quite a shock to Lord Phillip, too. Were they close?"

"Not really. Reggie was sort of a pompous malcontent who got on everyone's nerves, but not really a bad guy, I suppose. Jessica remembers only the good things now . . . the birthday parties when she was a little girl, how he would take her for walks, the presents at Christmas. He was a link to her mother, one that's lost forever now."

"It's a bad way to lose someone," Chief said, turning the wheel to avoid a buoy.

"The worst part of it was the lack of any sign. He seemed to be the same Uncle Reggie, as quarrelsome as ever. I didn't think he was the type to do himself in."

"That's something you can't tell, Ben. No one knows the devils people are wrestling inside."

Kane sighed and took in a deep breath of sea air. He filled his lungs and let it out slowly. He loved the spray of the sea, the cool wind in his face.

"How are we doing with Ganja?" he asked the Chief.

"I shut off the sound on that damn thing. It kept chirping along like a heartbeat and it was getting on my nerves. He hasn't run into any trouble yet."

Kane picked up the black box receiver from the shelf above the wheel. When the sound of the pulser was turned off, a small red light blinked every fifteen seconds. Even that was extraneous because it would sound an alarm the moment the energy cadence was changed. As long as Ganja didn't press the eyes on the crucifix transmitter, the shadow would keep a regular vigil.

Weaver had shown him how the square black box worked. Inside there was a series of concentric circles and a red and a white light. The red light

153

was Ganja, and the white light was the location of the Shadow. Each concentric circle represented fifteen hundred feet. Ganja could be located wherever he was transmitting from on the island by lining up the two circles of light.

He put the box back on the shelf, after noticing that the Leopard had already crossed one of the circle demarcations as it moved closer to Mica Island.

Ben stepped away from the Chief and went below. Miles was making them some coffee.

"I would have liked to bring some artillery with us," Miles told him.

Kane patted his S & W .357 magnum in his shoulder holster. "Do you have your .38?"

"Yeah."

"That should be enough," Kane said. "I'm not anticipating any real trouble. Ganja will look around, see what he can find, and then we'll get him off."

"Piece of cake, Skipper."

Ganja woke up with a start. The other two men weren't in the room. He looked at his watch. It was five-fifteen. Breakfast was served at five-thirty. He got dressed quickly and headed for the cafeteria.

Steve and George were sitting at the table and eating. They didn't acknowledge his presence.

"Hey, I'm sorry about last night, guys," Ganja said. "I know Major Frank must have said something to you."

Steve and George concentrated on finishing their eggs. They didn't turn in Ganja's direction.

"Okay, what is this? The cold shoulder? I said I was sorry."

There was no response.

Ganja shrugged and went to the tables. There were eggs and sausages or bacon, cold cereals, and a choice of milk, coffee, or tea. In spite of his resolve not to be doped by the food, his stomach was growling and he felt he needed to eat something. He helped himself to an unopened box of corn flakes and poured some milk into a bowl. He brought it back to the table.

"How did you guys sleep?" he asked them.

"Okay," Steve said in a monotone.

"How about you, George?" Ganja asked him.

For a second, George looked like he was going to say something, then he caught himself and continued chewing his food.

It was as if someone had caught his eye and warned him to keep quiet. Ganja turned to see if anyone was behind him giving George some kind of signal. There wasn't.

"What's the matter, George? You starting to become like them?" Ganja said, nodding his head in the direction of the fifty men who were eating their breakfast at the adjoining tables.

As soon as he said it, Ganja understood. It was

more than their reticence, it was their whole bearing. They were sitting straight up, backs against the chair backs. They ate their food using crisp quick jabs of their knives and forks. They chewed each mouthful a certain number of times before swallowing. Even their eyes had that same semi-glazed quality he had seen in the other Mica Security zombies.

Ganja realized he was sticking out like a sore thumb if anyone compared him to the two other new recruits. He started to copy them. He ate his food in silence and tried to mimic their precise manner. He kept his eyes down on his plate as he finished his bowl of cereal.

"How's it going here, men?"

Major Frank was standing at the head of their table looking at them.

"Very good, sir," the three of them answered.

"Good. I hope you all had a good night's sleep. That white noise sure takes away the tension of the day. It makes you get up ready to take on the world, doesn't it, men?"

"Yes, sir!"

"You two men carry on. Garrett, you come with me," Frank said.

Ganja stood up and tried to keep his face a blank mask. He followed Major Frank out of the cafeteria and down the hall to the Major's office.

"Sit down, Garrett!" he said gruffly.

Ganja took a chair opposite the Major's desk. Frank had pictures of Link Mica on the walls and the Mica industry banner behind his chair.

"Somebody here I want you to meet," Major Frank said.

He pushed a button on the console. In a moment, the door opened. Ganja turned in his chair. Jacob Peters was standing in the doorway.

"Yes, Major. That's the man," he said.

"Okay, you can go now," the Major grunted.

He stared at Ganja while Jacob closed the door behind him.

"Why did you go to talk to that man?" Major Frank asked him.

"I didn't, sir," Ganja answered.

Major Frank leaned back in his chair. He rubbed his eyes with the palms of his hands.

"Who sent you?"

"Nobody sent me, sir. I want to serve. I'm willing to work as one for the good of the many," Ganja parroted.

"This man, Peters, reported something strange this morning. He said that last night a man came into his room and started asking him questions about some woman who he never heard of, and where he was from, and things like that. Ring a bell?"

"No, sir."

"This happened around the same time that you had your supposed stomach attack. That's some coincidence."

"I think—"

"Now I bring him in here and he identifies you

157

as the same man who visited him last night. More of a coincidence?"

"Yes, sir."

"I don't think so. I think you're a spy, Nick Garrett, or whatever your name is. I want to know who sent you here. I want to know who is trying to stop Link Mica from bringing peace and happiness to the world."

"I can explain," Ganja said. "That man's girlfriend got worried about him. She believed he was going to come home, and when he signed up for another three months, she asked me to find out what happened. I admit that I came here under false pretenses. I'm sorry about that. Jacob Peters is obviously ill and he doesn't remember Sharon. It's as simple as that. So he signed up for another three months. It certainly wasn't against his will, as anyone can see." Ganja stood up. "I won't take up any more of your time. I'll leave the island right away and that will end the matter."

"Sit down!" Major Frank ordered. "There's a problem with your little story. You see, Link has many friends. Last night when you slipped up by calling the bathroom a head, I asked one of Link's friends in Washington to run a check on Nick Garrett. Do you want to know what we found? Well, let me tell you. It seems that Nick Garrett was in the Marine Corps, and did serve in Vietnam. But he died six months ago, in an automobile accident. That Nick Garrett served in Army Intelligence and, after the war, was a spook for the

Central Intelligence Agency."

"I took his identity in order to get a job on the island."

"You people disgust me!" Major Frank said. "If you only knew how important our mission is for mankind. Get out of here! Just get out of my sight!"

Major Frank pressed a button on the console. "I want this character out of my office!" he snapped.

A moment later, two of the Security men stepped into the room.

"Come with us," they droned.

Ganja stood up. "I can take your next boat to Charlotte Amalie."

He was walking to the door when he noticed a swift movement out of the corner of his eye.

The soldier behind him crashed a blackjack to Ganja's skull. Ganja fell to the floor in a heap.

CHAPTER 16

Weaver wanted answers. He paced his Ultratech office like a caged lion. What had started out as a quiet molehill had blossomed into an active volcano.

He was supposed to have a handle on everything that happened in his neck of the woods. He was the man with his finger on the pulse of the Virgin Islands. That's how he liked it. That's how he felt comfortable. Now he was feeling like he was on board a runaway locomotive, and he didn't like it.

"Mr. Willoughby to see you," the voice on the intercom said.

"Give him the usual," Weaver told the disembodied voice.

"The usual" meant to make a visitor wait for eight minutes. Not seven or nine, but precisely eight. Eight minutes made the person in the waiting room feel tense, but it wasn't long enough to foster resentment. The eight-minute rule always gave Weaver an edge. He would need it with Willoughby.

Willoughby was Sir Phillip Carlisle's personal secretary. At least that was his cover. In actuality, he was Weaver's counterpart in England's intelligence network, the FAI, Foreign Analysis and Information.

It would be hard to imagine a greater contrast than that between these two men. Willoughby, ferret faced with darting eyes, carrying a paunch on his small, cheaply clothed frame, and Weaver, tall, fit, wearing well-tailored clothes. Yet Weaver knew that Willoughby was every bit his equal in cunning and dedication to his work.

"I asked you here to compare notes, Willoughby. I want to know what you have on Link Mica," Weaver said pleasantly as Willoughby sat down.

"Why would we be interested in Mica?" Willoughby answered him. "He's an American, so he's your problem."

"He may be an American, but he's dealing with leaders the world over, including some from the British Empire, old man."

"I see, Mr. Weaver. But the fact is that we

English haven't had an 'empire' for quite some time."

"Are you going to deal with me, Willoughby, or are we going to have to step over each other's feet in order to find out what's going on?" Weaver said reasonably.

Willoughby thought over Weaver's offer. It was rare for the CIA man to call on him for help. They always tried to be so damned independent. American trait, he supposed.

"Why the interest all of a sudden? The Facility has been around a while now."

Weaver stood up and started pacing the floor again. "I don't like things I can't explain. That island has got me too much in the dark."

"You tried to plant someone, of course?"

"Yeah, but no luck. I had two good people, and they were both snuffed out. I just got word an hour ago that one of them, Ray Kupper, jumped off the top of the stateside hospital we had him in."

Willoughby's eyes opened for a second. "Hmmm. Suicide?"

"Yeah, suicide. Except Ray had been given the whole scientific mumbo-jumbo tests that said he definitely was not suicidal."

"Tests can be inaccurate."

"You think so? Check this out, old man."

Weaver walked over to the computer console. "On," he said in a slow, strong voice.

"Computer on," the machine responded.

"Statistical accuracy of Farraday-Courtney Personality Profile?"

"Point nine seven one six eight four."

"Accuracy in prediction of suicide?"

"Point nine nine four eight two."

"You can't get much better than that," Weaver said with a shrug.

"Reggie Thornton killed himself two days ago," Willoughby announced.

Weaver let it sink in. "Colonel Reggie? That's hard to believe. I wonder . . ."

He turned to the computer. "Employ all data banks and tell me how many of the people known to have been on Mica Island committed suicide."

"Six of fifty-two known to be on Mica Island," the voice synthesizer replied.

"Statistical probability of six out of fifty-two healthy adults committing suicide?" Weaver asked the computer.

"Point zero zero zero seven four six," was the response.

"Hear that, Willoughby?"

Willoughby shrugged. "You Americans love your gadgets, don't you? We don't need a talking computer to tell us that there's some queer business afoot."

Weaver ignored him. "Was there a note of some kind from Thornton?"

"Nothing. How about this Kupper chap?"

"No. There's got to be some tie-in," Weaver said, sitting down and running his hand through his short blond hair.

"Colonel Reggie was under fire in England for sponsoring an offshore oil lease to the Mica people which many felt put Her Majesty's government at a disadvantage. He didn't seem the type, though, to let some criticism bother him."

"You know, Senator Mike Palmer sponsored legislation granting Mica Industries special tax credits. He was one of Mica's guests."

"Yes. Even though we don't have your hardware, Weaver, we do know which way the wind blows."

"What's that supposed to mean?"

"We've just completed a study that's been verified by the Ministry. The results are most revealing. Every one of the people that we tracked to Mica's facility did something to help Mica Industries within one month after their return."

"Arthur Bradley wrote an article in the *Times* defending Mica's right to conduct genetic restructuring without interference from the Academy of Science. Anna Sterling, the actress, narrated a Mica fluff piece for the BBC. In your own country, Todd Postmas agreed to accept Mica Industries as a sponsor, even though his show had a waiting list of major corporations."

"Could it be simple gratitude?"

"I doubt it. These people aren't the types to gush over their cures."

Weaver tapped the desk. "Why haven't you done anything about Link Mica?" he queried his counterpart.

"I suppose for the same reason you haven't,"

Willoughby replied evasively.

"I've been ordered to back off."

"Precisely my situation."

Weaver stood up and walked to his map. He touched the blue glowing area that was the United States and put his index finger on Washington, D.C.

"You don't imagine . . ."

"I've thought about it, Weaver. It's hard to believe, but then again, it's not like the P.M. to stand in the way of an FAI investigation. It is possible that the P.M. himself could have been one of Link Mica's guests."

Weaver nodded. "This is between the two of us. I think you know that my director, Bucky Davis, had had a problem on occasion holding his Haig and Haig. There was a rumor that the President was going to replace him if he didn't shape up. I wonder . . ."

"At any rate, our hands are officially tied."

"What do you think Link Mica's up to? The man doesn't need to make any more money. He could never spend what he has."

"Power."

Weaver leaned forward and spoke seriously. "I've planted another man inside. I hope I have more success this time around."

"Can't you use those spy satellites you people are so fond of? At last count, you've shot up seven hundred of the things around the world."

Weaver shrugged. "If those things existed,

which I don't say they do, they can't see inside buildings."

"The ladies at my wife's bridge club will be happy to hear that, Weaver. I was thinking that perhaps these nonexistent pieces of equipment might enable us to get a better idea of who comes and goes at The Facility."

"Maybe that's how we came up with our fifty-two names," Weaver said. "Where did you get sixty-one?"

"We muddle through without any mechanical wizardry, I'm afraid. We just keep our dreary old lists."

"I'll show you mine if you'll show me yours," Weaver said.

"I think that might be arranged."

CHAPTER 17

Ganja's head throbbed. He was lying face down on a cold stone floor. He moved slowly, trying to escape the arrows of pain that coursed through his head as he lifted himself to a sitting position. His hands were tied behind his back. No, he wasn't tied, he was handcuffed. He looked down at his chest. At least they hadn't taken the crucifix transmitter. Although there was no way he could activate it, with his hands behind his back.

He surveyed his surroundings. He was in a small, white-painted cell with walls on three sides and bars on the fourth. A naked light bulb, high up on the ceiling, illuminated the room. There were no windows or furniture of any kind.

Looking through the bars, he could see three more cells directly opposite his. In one, a man was lying on the floor sleeping, or unconscious. Next to him, a light-skinned black man was moaning and banging his head against the bars. The third cell had an old woman who was making grotesque expressions and flailing clawed hands through the bars.

"Hey, over here!" Ganja called out to the other inmates. He tried to get their attention, but they were completely oblivious to him.

"They won't answer you," a female voice said.

It came from the right, just out of view of his cell. Ganja stood up and walked to that corner.

"They've gone crazy," the woman said. "Try to ignore them. Once they start to make a racket, it's impossible to sleep."

"Where are we?" Ganja asked.

He could see a little bit of her now. She seemed to be a young, attractive redhead. She was in the adjoining cell.

"It's the basement of the Security Building. I've been here for a week now. Who knows how long those other poor souls have been locked down here. Maybe they're the lucky ones. What did you do?"

"I was trying to find out some information."

The redhead laughed. "Welcome to the club," she said. "My name is Coco. What's yours?"

"Coco? You were on the island with the white slavers?"

"That's right. Who are you?"

"Ganja Grant. I work for Ben Kane. What are they going to do to us?"

"Expose us to correct thoughts. They strap you into a chair and put this contraption on your head and you listen to noises for hours on end. Those poor bastards over there got the early treatment. They gave them too much too soon, and it turned them into mindless animals. I'm the next generation of guinea pig. They're going slower with me. They still haven't gotten it right, though."

"What the hell are correct thoughts?"

"That's when you think like them. That's when you decide that your life is worth shit and everything that Link Mica does is great."

"Maybe it won't work at all. You seem to be okay."

"Except for the headaches, I don't feel much different." Coco admitted. "But they got something new now. They combine the white sound with electrical shock. It worked on some poor guy who—"

"Jacob Peters," Ganja said.

"Yeah, that's his name. They baked him for a couple of days and he popped out a convert. You know him?"

"His fiancée wanted me to find out why he didn't come back to her. They wiped out his memory."

"That explains why they haven't rushed to use the technique on me. If you lose your memory completely, you can't serve his Highness Link Mica to the utmost of your capabilities."

"Is there any way out of here?" Ganja asked.

"Sure, but I'm just hanging around because I enjoy having my brains scrambled," Coco answered with a short laugh. "You get one meal a day, it's not much but it will keep you going. You get taken out to use the bathroom once in the morning. You sleep during the day because they feel that your mind is more susceptible at night. Two guards watch you at all times, and they keep their guns aimed on you. If you could get through the bars and knock out the guards, you'd still have to break through a steel door at the top of the staircase . . . and get past a guard with a machine gun, on duty twenty-four hours."

"Shit!" Ganja said.

"My sentiments exactly. Let me tell you something else: These guards of Mica's are just semi-human. All they want to do is make sure they don't let down the rest of the Mica establishment. Keeping us from escaping is like part of their religion. I've tried a thing or two, and either they're totally committed—or they're castrated."

"Are you handcuffed?" Ganja asked her.

She extended her hands out through the bars. "I guess they don't think I could overpower them."

"Do you think you could reach into my cell over here?"

"Probably. Why?"

"Just reach into my cell and touch the crucifix on my chest."

"Whatever turns you on, lover, if it will get us out of here."

Coco reached over between the bars of his cell. By standing as close as he could, he could bring his chest near her fingers. She reached around blindly until she finally was able to feel the crucifix.

"Isn't this romantic?" she said.

"Feel the top. There are two little stones where the eyes are."

"I feel them. Do I make a wish?"

"Press in the right one and keep pressing it for five seconds, then do the same for the other stone."

"Okay, now what?"

"That's it. Now we wait for the cavalry to arrive."

Miles knocked on Ben Kane's cabin.

"They're playing our song, Skipper!" he called.

Kane sprang out of bed and joined Miles and Chief Bukowski in the pilothouse. The black Shadow box was giving off an ear-shattering alarm.

"Shut the damn thing, Ben," Bukowski yelled over the siren. "I can't hear myself think."

Kane picked up the box and looked for a shut-off

switch. He had forgotten to ask Weaver how to stop the alarm once it sounded. He turned it around and over, but he didn't see anything that looked like a switch.

Miles pulled out his .38. "I'll shut it off," he said.

"No, we'll need this."

Kane ran his fingers over the top of the box and found a soft spot. He pressed it down, and the sound stopped immediately.

"About time," Bukowski said, sticking his index finger in his ear and moving it around.

"Gun her, Chief. Mica's got his security boats in the water and we've got to get to the island before they can catch up to us."

"I'm building up a head of steam, Ben. We'll be near the beach in just a few minutes."

"I'll check the tarp," Miles told them.

The tarp was an invention of Kane's. He remembered in Nam how jungle camouflage canvas could hide a dozen tanks, and he realized that the same tactic could be used with boats. The tarp, painted the same color as the Caribbean Ocean, could be placed over the Sanger Alley Cat and for all intents and purposes be invisible from the shore or from the air.

"What do we have on the radar?" Ben asked Bukowski.

The Leopard had been outfitted with a Wesmar SR440. Bukowski had programmed in a fifteen-mile intrusion zone around the Leopard.

They watched the ten-inch screen. The variable range markers and the electronic bearing line were updated thirty times a second and stored in the Wesmar's computer brain to project a picture of target blips.

"This one is moving toward us," Bukowski said, pointing to a pip at the outer circle of their guard zone.

"What about this one?" Kane pointed to another pip coming from the opposite direction.

"Yeah. They're moving fast, but we're close to the island. You should be able to hide the speedboat in time."

"The tarp's set up," Miles told them, walking into the pilothouse.

"We should be seeing Mica Island any moment now," Bukowski said. "I'm going to take you in on the west side."

"Good idea," Kane agreed.

Bukowski nosed the Leopard close to the island. Kane and Miles secured the Sanger. They made sure their escape vessel was well hidden by the tarp. Although the water was deep close to shore, there was no swinging room, so they anchored bow and stern.

"The patrol boats are breathing down our necks," Bukowski shouted from the Leopard.

"Take off, Chief! We'll see you back at the Rainbow Keg tonight."

"Good luck!" he called.

Chief Bukowski was to play the fox and lure the

hounds, in the shape of Mica's Security fleet, away from the operation. He would lead Mica's cutters away from the island and head back to port, giving Ben and Miles a chance to free Ganja.

Miles made it to shore first. He looked back out to sea and tried to make out the camouflaged Alley Cat.

"If you didn't know where to look, you could miss it," Ben told him as he joined him on the sand.

They both heard the sound of the jeep at the same time. The only cover was a group of rocks not far from the shoreline. They darted for them and ducked down.

The jeep carried two of Mica's uniformed security men. They rode right down to the beach and along the shore.

"They'll spot our footprints," Kane told Miles. Sure enough, the jeep came to a dead halt at the spot where Ben and Miles had swum ashore.

One of the men picked up a walkie-talkie.

"We've got to stop him before he radios in our position," Ben said.

He took aim with the magnum and sent a shot over the men's heads. The guard dropped the walkie-talkie down, and they jumped off the jeep. They took cover behind the four-wheel-drive vehicle and aimed their M16s at the rocks where Ben and Miles were hiding. Their first shots ricocheted off the rocks with a pinging noise.

"They've got us pinned down here pretty good,"

Miles said grimly.

"Yeah, I know. And time is on their side," Ben answered, looking around.

The rocks extended into a jetty. It was possible to keep their cover all the way into the ocean.

"Lay down some cover fire, Miles. I'm going for a swim," Ben said.

Miles squeezed off four rounds as Ben ducked down and headed back toward the sea. Miles kept on firing each time the Mica people stuck their heads out from behind the jeep. They put their M16s on automatic and laid down a barrage.

Ben placed his magnum in the waterproof backpack of his wet suit and dived into the water. He swam against the current. When he looked up, he was fifteen yards behind the two men firing at Miles.

He came out of the water and circled behind them. He wasn't concerned about their hearing him, not with the racket their semi-automatics were making. He got within ten feet of them before he called to them to put down their guns.

The two guards were taken by surprise. They had no chance to shoot Kane with him standing on top of them, but still they whirled and fired. Ben sent a slug from the magnum into one of the men's chest. He fell to the ground, his gun discharging harmlessly into the air. The second guard dropped like stone, with one of Miles's thirty-eight slugs passing right through his body.

"I guess these guys don't know how to surrender," Miles said.

"Stupid waste," Kane said, shaking his head. He picked up the M16s. "Well, looks like we inherited their guns."

"Yeah, and their jeep, too."

Kane took out the Shadow box and turned it on. Ganja's blip was now less than a mile away. He then took out a translucent map and placed it over the concentric circles of the box. Weaver and the Ultratech geniuses had supplied Kane with a detailed map of Mica Island. By superimposing the map over the concentric circles on the box, they could pinpoint Ganja's location.

"The Security Building," Kane told Miles, putting his finger down on the spot where the blip representing Ganja blinked. "We better put on their uniforms."

Miles nodded.

Kane and Miles finished putting on the Mica uniforms and then climbed into the jeep. The terrain was bumpy until they came to the outer periphery of the seven white buildings that made up The Facility.

One of the Mica Security people was standing in the middle of the road, flagging them down. There was a group of five other men behind him at the edge of the road. Ben had the choice of going past them, but that would draw even more attention to them. He stopped the jeep and the security man walked over. Kane noticed he had sergeant stripes on his sleeve.

"You men just come from the beach?" The sergeant asked them.

"Yes, sir!"

"You see anything out of the ordinary?"

"No, sir!" Kane replied.

The sergeant looked at them closely. "You fellows should get your hair cut soon. Is that understood?"

"Yes, sir," Kane said.

"What's wrong with your pal over there? Doesn't he know how to talk?"

Out of the corner of his eye, Kane saw Miles's fingers tighten around the stock of the M16.

"Sore throat," Kane explained.

"Well, Boat Patrol reported a yacht sailing close to the shore. We chased it out of the island waters, but it looks like he was snooping around for something. When you go back out there, keep a sharp eye."

"Yes, sir!" Kane said.

He put the jeep in gear and rolled forward.

"Hold it right there!" the sergeant yelled.

Kane slammed on the brakes. The sergeant came running over to the jeep. Kane reached under his uniform and felt the reassuring heft of his magnum.

"I've got something for you, solider," the sergeant told Miles.

"Yeah?"

He reached into his pocket and pulled out a package of throat lozenges.

"Take what you need and give the rest back to me at mess tonight."

Miles looked at Kane. "Thanks, sir," he finally said to the sergeant.

Kane pulled away quickly from the knot of men on the road. They moved into a road on the center of The Facility. There were just a couple of jeeps on the grounds. Most of the people, guards included, were walking.

"I'm going to park the jeep," Kane said. "We stick out too much riding around."

Miles nodded. He pointed to a spot near a cluster of cottages. There was a sign that said SENIOR STAFF COMPOUND. Kane left the jeep near the sign.

He and Miles began walking toward a building that was the farthest down a tiled path with flowers and budding trees running along it. Whenever they encountered another Security guard, they averted their eyes. But it really wasn't necessary. The men on Mica's force walked past without a nod or an acknowledgment.

"That's it," Kane said, pointing to the last white building.

Ben took out the Shadow box and looked at it. He wanted to make sure that Ganja was still there. The two blips were practically on top of one another, so he knew he was in the right place.

They walked into the building and came to a hallway. To the left was the cafeteria, to the right a bunch of closed doors. They went to the right.

The first three doors said MAJOR FRANK: SECU-

RITY FORCES SPECIAL COMMANDER. The rest of the doors had other names.

Miles tapped Ben on the shoulder. There was one door that said RECORDS. They turned the knob and walked in quickly.

A man wearing the familiar uniform looked up from his desk. "Yes?"

"We need to look up some information," Ben told him.

"Who authorized you to come in here?" he wanted to know.

He was officer-candidate material, Kane thought, all spit and brass right up to his quarter-inch crewcut.

"Major Frank."

"What is this? Major Frank wouldn't send someone in to look up any records. He'd call me on the intercom."

The man reached for the phone on his desk, but Miles got there first. Miles seemed to just flick the back of his wrist in the other man's jaw, but the man was driven off his chair by the force of the blow.

"He'll be out for at least an hour," Miles told Kane.

"All right, let's move quickly. Look for a file in the name of Nick Garrett. He might be in that one over there, the file that says New Recruits."

Ben thumbed through a bunch of folders in the file cabinet while Miles looked up "Garrett" in the new recruit roster.

"Here it is, Ben," Miles said, holding up some papers. "He's in room 206."

Kane looked around the room. There was a small closet with a number of very old typewriters piled one on top of the other. Ben took the typewriters out of the closet and put the information officer inside instead. He closed the door and pushed the typewriters up against it.

"Let's go!" he said to Miles.

They walked up the stairs and got to the second floor. The numbers went in sequence, and they immediately came to 206.

They knocked on the door and a voice said to come in. The man sitting at the small writing desk wasn't Ganja. He was a tall, dark-haired man with oily skin.

"Yeah?"

"Where's Nick Garrett?" Kane asked him.

The man shrugged. "I haven't seen him since they took him away this morning."

"Who took him away?" Miles asked gruffly.

"Major Frank."

They thought about that.

"You have any idea why Major Frank wanted to separate him from the unit?" Ben asked.

"Somebody said that he was a spy. I guess you'd better check with the Major."

"Right. We'll do that," Ben told him.

They walked out the door of the dorm and down the hall.

"Now what?" Miles grunted.

"Major Frank. He's the only one who knows where Ganja is. No sense wasting our time with anybody else," Kane decided.

Ben and Miles went back to the suite of offices with Major Frank's name on the door. They walked through the door into an outer office where an official-looking male secretary was placing some papers into a desk drawer.

"Yes?"

"We want to see the Major," Ben said.

The secretary's eyes narrowed. Obviously, the guards in the Mica Security Forces didn't barge into the Major's office and ask to see him.

"What's this all about?"

"We'd like to talk to the Major. It's something that he should know."

"Personal," Miles added.

The secretary looked across the room to another door with a green frosted window. "He's in conference right now, but you have to go through your sergeant and then up the chain of command to see him."

Kane nodded, then clipped the secretary with a hard right cross.

The man fell sideways into Miles's arms. They put him on the floor behind his desk and walked over to the door with the frosted glass. They could hear voices on the other side, but it was impossible to make out what was being said.

Miles tried the doorknob, but it was locked.

"Kick it in," Ben told him, setting up the M16 in

the crook of his arm.

Miles smashed the door with his heel. It smashed back into the wall.

Three men, all in uniform, were sitting at a conference table. Another man, well over six feet, was standing in front of a map of the island complex. He had a pointer in his hand, and from his uniform, Ben and Miles figured him to be Major Frank.

"Nobody move!" Miles said, leveling the M16 in their faces.

"What the hell is this?" Major Frank exploded. "Who are you men?"

"You've got a pal of ours. We've come to collect him," Ben said.

"I don't know what the hell you're talking about."

"Nick Garrett, where is he?" Kane demanded.

Major Frank started laughing. "Do you think you're going to get anything out of me or my people?"

"If you want to live, you'll cooperate."

"You can't intimidate us," one of the men seated at the table said.

"You just tell us where our friend is and everybody can carry on."

"Shoot us, then," Major Frank said, putting his hands behind his back. "I'd gladly give my life for Link Mica and what he stands for."

The men sitting around the table all voiced agreement.

"We'll be martyrs for the cause gladly," one of them said.

Miles put the muzzle of his gun against the Major's throat.

Frank pushed it away disdainfully. "One death is meaningless so the many can survive."

It was obvious to Ben that Major Frank wasn't bluffing. He had seen the Mica Security Forces march right into a machine-gun nest on Pelican Cove.

He decided to try something else. "Link Mica is going to consider you a traitor," Ben told him.

"What are you talking about?"

"You betrayed him."

"That's a lie. I will never betray my commander!"

"You're willing to die to protect the whereabouts of one man. You'll die and all of your troops will be without their leader. Mica will be without his trusted right arm. Your foolish attempt at bravery will deprive the movement of one of its most important leaders."

Miles looked at Ben Kane as if he had gone crazy, too.

Major Frank, however, was deep in thought.

"He's right, Major," one of the men at the table said. "You're too valuable to be lost because of this."

"Give them their friend," another one said.

"It's up to you, Major Frank. Do you die for nothing, or is Link Mica's work too important?"

Ben wheedled.

"Link Mica's work must never be stopped," Major Frank said, wrestling with himself.

"We just want our friend," Kane prodded.

"Damn it! Then come with me," Major Frank grumbled.

"What about them, Ben?" Miles asked, looking at the three officers at the conference table.

"I'm ordering you men to stay at this table until I come back. Is that clear?" Frank boomed.

"Yes, sir!" they answered as one.

"I'm going to put the M16 on my shoulder, Major, but I'm still covering you with this." Ben held up the magnum.

"Understood," Major Frank said curtly.

He walked in front of Miles and Kane down the corridor and past the cafeteria. Kane was surprised to see there was another wing to the building that, because of its architecture, wasn't obvious from the outside. At the end of this corridor, a guard sat with a machine gun on his lap.

All the way around the building people saluted the Major, who saluted back. Everyone seemed oblivious to Miles and Kane. It appeared that they were accompanying the Major on some tour.

The guard with the machine gun stood at attention. Behind him, Kane saw a steel door with a KEEP OUT warning.

"Open the door for us, Brewster," Frank commanded.

The man put down his machine gun and tapped in a series of numbers on a keypad on the side of the door. It opened slowly, revealing a long staircase.

Miles pulled his .38 from his shirt and held it on the guard.

"Let's go, pal," Ben told him. "You're joining our parade."

CHAPTER 18

Ganja was led out of his cell by the two silent Security guards Coco had told him about. One held a pistol on Ganja, while the other one opened the cell door and pushed Ganja out.

"They're going to measure you for one of their thinking caps," Coco told him. "Don't worry about it. The fun will start tonight."

"I can't wait," Ganja said wryly.

They pushed him along, past the cell block area, to a steel door. One man tapped in a code on a keypad, and the door swung open. Ganja didn't like what he saw. It looked like the laboratory of

Dr. Frankenstein. In the center of the room was a large wooden chair. A gizmo on the top of the chair made Ganja think of the driers that women used in a beauty parlor, but the arm and leg clamps drove that thought from his mind in a hurry.

"Sit down, please."

Ganja turned to see where the voice was coming from.

A tall, stern-faced man with a black goatee, wearing a white lab coat, motioned for him to sit in the chair of honor. When Ganja hesitated, one of the two guards behind him gave him a love tap in the kidney. It convinced Ganja that sitting in the hot seat wasn't such a bad idea after all.

"Who are you?" Ganja asked the goatee.

"I'm Dr. Hannon. I'm helping Link with his work."

"What are you going to do to me?"

"Please don't be alarmed. No one will hurt you. Right now we are going to take some measurements of your skull so we can equip you with a cranial device that will assist you in achieving correct thoughts."

"Like the way you assisted Jacob Peters, or those other poor bastards in their cells?"

"That happened before I came here . . . before Link asked me to assist him. As for Jacob Peters, he's perfectly fine."

"Sure, a man whose memory is wiped out and who's suffering from terrible headaches every hour—he's in tip-top shape."

Hannon's face twisted in anger. He slapped Ganja hard across the face. "Shut up!"

Ganja strained against the clamps without any success.

"Don't make things harder for yourself," Hannon warned. "The longer you try to resist, the more painful the sessions will be."

He took what looked like forceps and made measurements of Ganja's head. He wrote down his figures in a small black notebook.

"There, that just about—"

There was a slamming sound, evidently coming from above them.

"Check that out!" Hannon ordered the guards.

One guard disappeared behind a small door at the end of the laboratory.

Ganja looked around him. There were two very large computers and a table set up with different color beakers. Two very thick cables, looking like elephant trunks, descended from the ceiling. One hooked up to one of the computers, the other cable plugged into what looked like a very large stereo speaker. From the other side of the speaker a snakelike cable emerged and went into the apparatus on top of the chair he was sitting in.

"What is this stuff supposed to do to me?"

"Help you," Hannon said casually.

The door opened and in stepped the guard, with his hands up in the air. The guard from the first floor came next, and then Major Frank. Kane and Miles took up the rear.

"What is this?" Hannon asked, his eyes popping open.

"Put down your gun, soldier!" Major Frank commanded.

The guard did as he was told. The gun fell to the floor with a dull thud.

"Now get him out of that chair!" Ben told him.

The guard looked over to Major Frank, who nodded.

He opened Ganja's clamps, and the black man bent over and picked up the gun on the floor. He walked over to Hannon and slapped him hard across the face. Hannon put this hand to his cheek and cowered.

"I was beginning to wonder if you guys were going to show up," Ganja said.

"We got here as fast as we could," Kane told him. "What were they going to do, straighten your hair, Ganja?"

"Something like that."

"Let's get these guys locked up; then get out of here." Kane said.

Ganja pushed the two guards ahead of him and made one open the steel door to the cell block. The three insane prisoners began screaming at the top of their lungs when they saw Ganja bring in the guards. They jumped up and down and smashed themselves against the bars in a frenzy.

"Coco!" Kane said.

"Ben Kane!" Coco yelled from across the room.

"What the hell are you doing here?" Kane asked

her.

He reached into the guard's pocket, took out the cell keys, and let Coco out.

"Am I glad to see you guys!" she said. "They were going to brainwash us, and then the world. Link Mica sends the signals over to this island with that transmitter on his ship. We've got to get to him before it's too late."

They herded the guards, Hannon, and Major Frank into one cell.

"What about them?" Ganja asked, pointing to the three people screeching and jumping like animals.

"It's too late for them," Coco said sadly.

"I'm afraid she's right," Kane said. "Come on!"

He retraced his steps, back through the lab and up the steps to the first floor.

"Miles, you walk in front of them and I'll take the back. We'll make it look like they're our prisoners and we've got orders to take them somewhere."

Miles trotted in position.

They passed through the Security Building and out without any trouble. As they walked along the tiled path, they sensed that something was going on. A guard speaking into a walkie-talkie moved into their path.

"Just a second!" he said.

Miles's hands moved so quickly it seemed they were a blur. One second the guard was standing ominously in front of them. The next moment, he was lying on the ground out cold.

"They're on to us," Kane said. "Double-time it!"

He broke into a run. They were only twenty yards away from the jeep. Between them and the vehicle, however, were four more of the Mica guards. These four didn't seem to have a walkie-talkie. They seemed to be at ease, walking slowly and thinking to themselves.

"Go by easy," Kane said. "These four aren't on to us, let's not blow it now."

They moved back into a slow walk and passed the knot of guards without their looking up.

"Almost home free now," Kane said, getting aboard the jeep.

They started the engine and began to move past the Senior Staff cottages. A woman walked by, and Ben almost stopped when he saw the familiar face of Karen Aztec. She looked at him for a second, her face breaking into a smile, and then a confused look.

Suddenly she stepped back and recoiled. "Stop them! Stop them!" she screamed.

The guards who had been walking by moments before turned.

"Shit, Ben! They're turning their guns on us," Ganja warned.

"Hold on tight, everybody," Ben said.

He floored the pedal on the jeep and the vehicle shot forward. A volley of shots rang out behind him. Kane headed for the beach. Soldiers on the road turned as he whizzed by, but they weren't aware of what was happening.

"Everybody okay?" Ben called back.

There wasn't any answer. Kane turned around for a second, and saw Ganja and Miles holding Coco between them.

The girl's body was lifeless. A drop of bright red blood ran down the edge of her mouth.

Ben changed gears and drove the jeep as close as possible to the shoreline. He spotted the jetty he had used for cover, and there lying in the sand were the two bodies of the Mica people.

"Over there," Miles said, pointing to the spot where the camouflaged speedboat should be. Even Ben had trouble seeing it at first. The tarp blended in perfectly with the color of the water. The only thing missing was the roll and pitch of the waves.

Ganja was the last to leave the jeep. He placed Coco's body down on the front seat and covered her with the shirt of his Mica uniform. Kane tied her foot to the gas pedal and positioned her body so her weight would push it down. The jeep began moving along the beach. He hoped it would draw Mica's people away from them.

"Let's go, Ganja," Ben said gently.

"Yeah," Ganja answered. He turned his back on the dead girl and, without looking back, ran into the water.

They waded out as far as they could, holding their guns above the waves. Halfway to the Sanger Alley Cat, Miles handed his weapon to Kane to protect it from the water, and swam to the boat.

As Miles reached the tarp and started to peel it back, they heard the drone of something close by.

"That's a chopper!" Kane exclaimed.

"Sounds like more than one," Ganja said, looking around to search the sky.

"Quick, under the tarp," Kane said, holding it up over his head until Ganja and Miles joined him.

They were able to hold on to the boat with one hand while they waited for the helicopters to pass.

"Shit, they're right on top of us!" Ganja said.

Indeed, the sound of the rotors seemed to be only feet away, as if the choppers were going to land right on top of them. For one brief instant, Kane thought that they had been discovered. The choppers weren't moving away. He braced himself for the onslaught of machine-gun bullets that would rip through the tarp and cut them all to shreds.

Then the sound of the choppers lessened.

"They're moving away," Miles said.

They lifted the tarp and looked out from underneath. The pilots had seen the jeep moving slowly along the shoreline and were following it.

There were two choppers. They weren't the ones Kane had seen on Pelican Cove. Those had been basically troop transporters, big jobs with little firepower. The two gunships in the air now were designed for one purpose: to hunt and kill. They were UH-1X Dragonflies, turbo-props armed with rockets, twin machine guns, and 40mm Bofors guns. They were capable of firing 18,000 rounds of ammunition a minute, with a range of five hundred miles and a maximum cruising speed of 250 miles an hour.

Getting back to Barracuda Reef was going to be a problem.

"Let's go," Kane commanded.

They ripped off the tarp and climbed into the Cat. Ben started her up, and the three men were pushed back in their specially padded seats as the jet engines thrust forward with 1000 horsepower. The needle on the speedometer nosed up to 107 mph within seconds.

Miles turned around, scanning the horizon for the deadly Dragonflies.

"You see anything, Miles?" Kane yelled over the roar of the PT-8 helicopter turbine.

"Nothing, Commander."

"Maybe they're on the other side of the island," Ganja said.

"Uh, oh. Here comes trouble."

Kane saw the cutter in the distance. It had obviously been alerted to intercept any boat coming from the island.

"Yeah, and it's loaded with big guns. What do we do, Skip?" Ganja said.

"We'll outrun her to the open sea," Kane said. "As long as the engine puts out, we shouldn't have to worry."

The water exploded twenty feet in front of them.

"They've got long-range bazookas!" Ganja said.

Another explosion in the water, this time just behind them.

"Hang on to something!" Kane yelled.

He started a zigzag motion with the Cat. Two other shells hit the water, but the Sanger was pulling out of range fast.

"All right!" Ganja said triumphantly, leaning over to give the speedy Cat a grateful pat.

"Another ten minutes and we'll be in the major sea lanes. If we keep this speed, we'll be back on Barracuda within the hour."

"Look out there," Miles said, pointing behind him to an insect-like spot on the horizon.

"What is it?" Kane asked him.

Ganja turned around and looked where Miles was pointing. "Shit! Here comes the Dragonfly!"

CHAPTER 19

After punching the key code to open his cell, Major Frank radioed the chopper pilot to pick him up from the roof of the Security Building. He personally wanted to track down the bastards who had eluded his forces and made a shambles of his operation.

He had been fooled for a moment by the girl in the jeep. When he realized that she was a decoy, he fired a 2.75-inch rocket from the mounted XM-3 system. The jeep exploded into an orange fireball.

He had to give them credit in spite of his anger. These people had a well-planned escape. He had

gotten the report from the Mica 108 that they had
outmaneuvered the much slower cutter in some
kind of hi-tech speedboat. The 108 had just missed
them with its bazookas, and they couldn't keep up
with the smaller boat's speed. Well, they might
have had it made, but they didn't reckon with the
UH-1X.

"How fast are we going?" he asked the pilot.

"Two thirty-four, Major."

"Well, go for the maximum. We have to find
those bastards before they get to the main sea
lanes."

"Yes, sir. I think I've got a fix on them on the
radar."

The pilot pointed to a spot on the edge of the
screen. "That's them," he said. "They're doing
over a hundred miles per hour."

"Are you going to catch them?"

"No problem. We're cutting our distance every
second."

"Good."

"We should have a visual fix on them about now,
sir. Yes, look over there at five o'clock."

Major Frank could see what the chopper pilot
meant. He couldn't see the boat itself, just a white
snowball of spray that the boat's engines were
kicking back.

Major Frank wrapped his big hands on the
triggers of the twin machine guns. The Dragonfly
could literally set the ground on fire with the
concentrated power of its machine guns. He

wouldn't have to aim very carefully. A powerboat like the one they were chasing was really a floating gas tank.

"We're going to be moving in behind them in just a minute."

"They still have their rifles," Major Frank said. "Be careful they don't get a good shot at you."

The pilot smiled. "The only thing that can bring us down is an armor-piercing shell. Nothing can crack this baby's skin, sir."

"Then take me in real close," the Major said.

The small craft was practically below them now, shooting back a mountainous spray of water.

The Major squeezed the trigger and enjoyed watching the line of his own bullets kick up their own spray as it inched closer to the back of the speedboat.

"Now you die!" the Major said, and he raked the Cat with bullets.

He saw wood splinter, and then the boat exploded, as the jeep had only minutes ago. This time he watched as the sky was flooded with debris. Something actually flew up and grazed the side of the chopper.

Major Frank laughed. "Look at that," he said, surveying the bright yellow-and-orange glow beneath them. "I bet some of that boat was blown a mile away."

"They had to be vaporized," the pilot said. "No one could live through that."

"Go back and let me rake the ocean."

"But—"

"Don't argue with me, son. I'm not taking any chances."

The pilot turned and moved back over the flaming wreckage. He hovered there as Major Frank spent the next ten minutes discharging the machine guns into the churning water.

When he was satisfied that nothing could have escaped alive, the Major motioned for the pilot to take them back.

The three men held on to a piece of wood from the Cat and treaded water. The boat's white paint had been stripped away by the force of the explosion. They had all thanked their lucky stars that they had jumped off long before the Dragonfly had gotten close enough to see them. It seemed like a good choice when they saw the Cat blown out of the water and the chopper hovering to make sure they were dead.

"How long have we been floating out here?" Ganja asked.

Kane looked at his watch. "I think between five and six hours."

"I thought this was a well-traveled route, Skip," Ganja said.

"I thought so too. But we haven't seen anything that even remotely resembles a boat."

Ganja massaged a cramp in his shoulder. "I feel

bad for Coco," he said. "She was a good kid."

"What was she doing there?" Kane asked him. "The last time I saw her, she was buddying up to Link Mica. She seemed to know how to attract powerful men. Her old boyfriend was Kalaxis."

"Kalaxis? You mean the shipping tycoon?"

"That's who I mean, Ganj. I think there was more to our friend Coco than met the eye."

Despite the conversation, Ben's mind was on Karen Aztec. He remembered how she had looked at him when she saw him. She had started to smile, and then it was as if she realized that she was doing something wrong.

Karen was more than just a pretty woman, Kane knew. She was a trained psychologist and a person with a well-developed sense of right and wrong. It was incredible that Mica could bend her to his will like that. Ben wished he could block out the sound of her voice alerting the guards that they were "spies."

"Skip, wake up!" Ganja was shaking him.

"What? What is it?"

"Listen," Miles whispered.

Ben thought he heard something over the lapping of the water. He shut his eyes and picked up the sound of an engine.

"Sounds like a boat," he said hopefully.

"No," Ganja shook his head.

"What then?" Miles asked him.

"Damn! It's a chopper!" Kane said.

"It's a chopper, all right. But different from that

warship of Mica's," Ganja told them.

"Well, what do we do, Skip?" Miles asked him.

"Like Ganja said, let's wave at the damn thing and hope it's over quick."

"Karen, are you all right?" Link Mica asked her.

He had come to her cottage and asked if he could come in. She was seated at her kitchen table drinking a cup of coffee. She tried to smile at Link, but she found that she couldn't stop crying. That was very odd. She couldn't figure out why she was crying.

"Yes, I'm fine, thank you."

"You seem very upset."

"Do I? I do feel . . . odd."

"Well, I don't blame you one bit. It must have been quite a shock to see Kane and his marauders riding through our peaceful island, trying to start trouble. When I heard about it, I had to come down and find out if they hurt you."

She listed to Mica and tried to understand what he was saying. "Why would Ben Kane want to hurt me? He's my friend."

"I thought he was my friend, too. I had no idea he'd try to kill me. I had him on my boat. Why, I even shared dinner with the man." Mica shook his head in sadness.

"He wanted to kill you? But that would have

destroyed everything. Only you can bring peace and happiness to the world, Link. Nothing must happen to you."

"Thank you, Karen. We're all in this together. We all have to work hard for the many."

"Ben Kane wouldn't hurt me," Karen said.

"I think he wanted to, Karen. I really think he wanted to kill those people who mean the most to our plan for humanity. People like Robert Townsend, and—"

"What happened to Robert?" Karen asked. "They didn't—"

"I'm afraid Robert's dead. I'm sorry. I thought you knew. Kane and his men killed him."

Karen seemed to be in shock. "Robert . . . dead . . . ?"

"Yes, and God knows how many others."

"I can't believe that Robert Townsend is dead," she said.

"Robert would have wanted you to carry on. Karen, do you hear me? I want you to take Robert's place as head of The Facility."

"Link, I can't. I can't replace a man like Robert Townsend."

"Yes you can. Your credentials are impressive, and you were a student of his. I know it's what Robert would have wanted."

"I don't know what to say. I seem to have this problem concentrating today. And, I'm crying for no reason at all."

"You don't have to give me an answer now. Just

think about it, okay?"

"What happened to Kane?" she asked.

"You don't have to worry about them anymore. Major Frank took care of them. We are free to continue our work without fear for our lives."

"That's a relief, Link."

"All right, then. Perhaps in a day or two you'll join me on *The Loyalty* and we'll discuss it further."

She let him out of the cottage and went back to her cold cup of coffee. How terrible that Robert Townsend was dead. And that Ben Kane had killed him. Could she take over for Townsend? And why would Ben kill Robert? So many things didn't make sense.

She should have been happy that Link asked her to take Robert's place. She should be happy that Kane and his men were killed. Then why was she crying?

Her hands were shaking and she felt out of control. There was no reason for it. It should have been a very happy day.

If she didn't stop feeling like this, she would just kill herself.

"Well, it doesn't have that damn Mica logo," Kane said, looking up at the chopper coming toward them.

"There is something written on the belly,

though." Ganja tried to make it out. "I don't believe it!"

"What?" Miles asked.

"It's Brand X Airways!" Ganja waved his arms frantically.

Brand X was the company their friend Henry Brand had started only a few months ago. Henry had had a small helicopter charter service and he moonlighted by doing some ferry work for Weaver. Ben recommended Henry to any of his charter patrons who needed a chopper to island hop. Henry had done so well with Kane's added business, he wanted to expand. With a loan from Caribbean Dream, Henry Brand now had six choppers and a successful company he named Brand X.

"Henry! Over here!" Kane hollered.

The chopper spotted them and moved in closer. In the chopper's glass-enclosed cabin, Kane could see Henry with his N.Y. Mets baseball cap, a woman sitting next to him.

Brand hovered over them and threw down the flotation collar. They all held on to it and let the chopper's winch take them up slowly.

Chief Bukowski was standing in the helicopter's doorway. He reached down and helped each of them into the chopper. Kane hadn't realized how exhausted they all were. He, Miles, and Ganja just lay on the floor of the chopper, trying to regain feeling in their arms and legs.

"Look at the three of you!" Bukowski scolded. "We're searching the ocean and you're off taking a pleasant little swim."

Ben closed his eyes. When he opened them, he smelled strong coffee and a perfume that was familiar.

"Drink some of this," Jessica said. "It will warm you up." She knelt down and gave them all steaming mugs.

"How did you find us?" Kane finally asked.

"I'll show you," Bukowski told him. He disappeared back into the chopper.

"Good afternoon, gentlemen. How are you three boys doing?" Henry Brand said, looking down on them.

"Hey! Get back in your chair and fly this thing!" Ganja yelled.

"It's okay, Ganj. I've got it on automatic pilot."

"You can't know how happy we were to see you, Henry," Kane said seriously.

"We're pretty happy to see you guys ourselves. We saw bits and pieces of the Alley Cat strewn all over the Atlantic. We had no idea if we were going to find you alive or in pieces."

Bukowski walked back to Kane and knelt down. "When I got back to port I called Weaver and asked him for another one of these, just in case." He held up the Shadow black box. "It was the same one you had tuned to the frequency on Ganja's crucifix. I just had Henry follow the bouncing ball."

"Chief, you earned your pay for the month," Kane said. "Now, what about Mica?"

CHAPTER 20

Henry Brand lowered the chopper lightly onto the painted circle of his helicopter pad outside Hangar 6 on Charlotte Amalie. It was the Brewers Bay side of the airport's new fifteen-hundred-foot extension, and for most of the week, the hangar office was only visited by people wanting to charter a Brand X helicopter.

Henry opened the doors and let Jessica out first. The men followed immediately. Kane and Ganja stretched their aching muscles. Miles seemed to be completely back to himself.

"How do you feel, Ben?" Bukowski asked him.

"I'll be fine just as soon as I walk around a bit," Kane said.

"Let's go into my office. I've got a bottle in the top drawer that may do more than exercise to help you to feel better," Brand said, grinning. "Hey, this guy looks like he's lost."

A huge Peterbilt eighteen-wheeler, advertising Coca-Cola on its sides, drove toward them. The driver rode right up to the chopper and rolled down his window.

"You're Henry Brand, right?" the driver asked.

He was an American black, wearing a blue workshirt with cut-off sleeves, revealing impressive biceps.

"Who wants to know?" Brand shot back.

"Ben Kane is with you, right?"

Kane and Brand exchanged glances.

"Maybe," Kane told him. "What's this all about?"

"I got to have an answer first. I need to talk to Ben Kane."

Suddenly, the man turned his head away. When he turned back, Miles was pointing a gun at his head. He had opened the door on the other side of the cab and taken the driver by surprise.

"Ask him why he's got an Uzi on the seat next to him," Miles yelled to Kane.

"Is that standard issue for Coca-Cola drivers? You involved in some kind of price war with Pepsi?" Kane asked him.

The driver measured his words. "If I wanted to

do you dudes in, you'd be dead already. Just because this guy has my gun at my temple doesn't mean I don't have to have an answer to my question."

"Yeah, I'm Ben Kane."

"Fine. If you go round to the back, there's a man inside the truck wants to talk to you."

"Who?" Ganja asked.

The driver shrugged, and pressed a button on the dash. The back of the truck opened.

They walked to the back and climbed the collapsible staircase that descended as the back doors opened. It was amazing how large the inside of the truck was.

They walked into what looked like a typical office waiting room, equipped with a color TV and magazines. A statuesque brunette, with a professional smile, greeted them. She was Suzy, Weaver's personal secretary.

"Ben Kane, how good it is to see you again." She extended her hand, which Kane shook.

Suzy never seemed to change. She was always perfectly coiffed, always tailored to the minute. The perfect front person for Weaver.

"I don't know some of you, I'm afraid. Miss Carlisle, of course. And the Chief. You two must be Ganja and Miles." She looked puzzled when she came to Henry.

"Henry Brand," he helped her.

"Of course. If I'm not mistaken, you've been very helpful to Ultratech over the years. Mr.

211

Weaver appreciates it, of that you can be sure."

"I never figured Weaver to appreciate anything," Ben told her.

Suzy laughed and shook her head. "Ben Kane, you know how much the Director thinks of you, and I have a pretty good idea that the feeling is mutual, in spite of your kidding."

"I can't put one past you, Suzy," Kane replied. "How long do we have to wait?"

"Just about four more minutes. How about a cup of coffee, or a drink?"

"So this is how my tax money gets spent," Kane said, looking around and noticing a video camera on the far wall.

"Hi, Weaver," he said, waving at the camera.

"Ohh, Mr. Kane!"

"Suzy, please send them in." Weaver's voice came out of a small speaker near the top of the office door.

Suzy grinned. "There we are. Please follow me."

They walked through an outer office, set up for Suzy and another girl, who was busy on a word processor and didn't look up. Then came the pantry and, as Suzy had said, an impressively stocked wet bar. Weaver's office door was closed and Suzy tapped on it lightly.

"Please, come in."

Suzy opened the door and held it for them until they all got into the room, then she gave a little good-bye wave and closed it behind her.

The office was very modern, with black space-age plastic furniture, gray plush carpeting, recessed lights, and hi-tech electronic maps on the wall with little lights blinking on and off all over the place. There was a large IBM computer on his desk, and on the wall opposite where Ben was standing, a bank of television monitors.

Weaver stepped away from his desk and motioned for them all to sit on a mauve crushed-velvet modular sofa. He drew up a small leather chair, which left him on a higher level.

"Damn good to see you made it out of there! I was really worried that you'd have some big trouble," Weaver told them.

"Actually, we ran into a few snags," Kane said. "We had to break Ganja out of Mica's prison."

"Prison?"

"I think Ganja should fill you in."

Ganja related the story to Weaver. The head of Ultratech listened intently and asked pertinent questions. He seemed amazed at the steps Link Mica had taken.

Ben was happy that Ganja hadn't said anything about Karen Aztec's part in their escape. Weaver's eyes came alive when Ganja mentioned Coco.

"Did you know her?" Ben asked Weaver.

"Yes, she was an independent contractor whose real name was Anna Malik."

"A Russian?"

"We were never quite sure. We know she had worked for the Russians, but she also worked for

213

us. Her allegiance was to money."

"Where does Robert Townsend come in?" Weaver asked with a concerned look on his face.

"We never saw him," Ganja said.

"What? Are you sure?"

"Of course we're sure, Weaver. We told you everything that happened. Why?"

Weaver leaned back and closed his eyes. He brushed his closely cropped blond hair with his palm. Kane recognized it as a mannerism Weaver used when he was trying to figure something out.

"Is there some problem with Dr. Townsend?" Jessica prodded.

"You might say so. He's dead."

"Dead!"

"Yeah. A bulletin went over the wires that Nobel Prize–winner Robert Townsend was killed in an attack of political fanatics. It then went on to say that Benjamin Kane, wealthy Virgin Island businessman, and two of his commandos were killed by Mica Security Forces while trying to escape."

"You've got to go to the authorities, Ben, and explain what really happened," Jessica pleaded.

"She's right, Ben," Chief Bukowski said, looking at his friend.

"No! That would be a terrible mistake." Weaver got up and began pacing. "As soon as you surface, as soon as anyone knows you're still alive, you'd be thrown into jail. This Mica thing extends very high up the ladder of governments around the world. There's no telling how far Mica has reached with his brainwashing techniques. I won't be able to lift a finger for you, Ben. My hands are tied. I wish I knew how he did it."

"When I was on *The Loyalty*, they made a big point of not letting anyone near this so-called Communications Room," Ben said. "Mica had this weird-looking antenna facing the direction of Mica Island. We were told that it was a new kind of receiver that could pick up communications from Mica's subsidiaries around the world. I thought that was kind of strange at the time, because the dish was facing south, toward Latin America rather than the States or Europe. Most of Mica's companies are in highly industrialized nations."

"What was in the room?" Weaver asked impatiently.

"I never found out, but Coco told us it was some sort of powerful transmitter."

"You mean, when people on the island put on their headphones to get that white noise, they were really being brainwashed by Mica's transmitter?" Ganja asked.

"It would be simple for Mica to override the signal that was being put out on the island with his own signal. Mica is a genius. He probably found a way to to stimulate brain waves to make people do whatever he wants."

"Why didn't he set it up right on the island?" Weaver asked.

"He probably needs the computer power he has aboard *The Loyalty* to make it work," Ben ex-

215

plained. "Also, he knew that Townsend wouldn't tolerate anything like that going on. People were coming to Mica's facility originally because of the stature of Robert Townsend. Mica certainly wouldn't do anything to make him suspicious."

Weaver thought it over. "That's it, then! We wipe out the transmitter, and we wipe out Link Mica."

He turned to the console on his desk and pushed a few buttons. An electronic map of the Virgin Islands formed on a screen in the wall to the right.

"The red light in the center of the map is Mica's boat, *The Loyalty*. He's got his own boats circling around for protection. Those are all the little white lights. We count on him having at least ten cutters and six good-sized cruisers. They've thrown a net around *The Loyalty* with some very sophisticated radar manufactured by Link's own outfit. I can't see any way to get close enough to do any damage to that transmitter."

Kane sighed. "I'm too tired to think. Maybe somebody in the Pentagon has a gizmo that can sneak us through Mica's radar."

"Hey, buddy boy, no one is going to help us with this thing. Link Mica is the world's fair-haired boy, and if I should say something to someone who turns out to be one of Link's converts, my next assignment will be in Siberia."

Kane shrugged. "Well, then let's sleep on it."

"No time, Ben. Mica's plans are starting to take shape. We've got to stop him right away or be prepared to become part of his slave empire."

"Why the rush all of a sudden?" Ganja asked him.

Weaver cradled his head in his hands. When he looked up, his face seemed drawn and tired.

"We received word a few moments ago that the Undersecretary of State will be here tonight in order to meet with Link Mica. A meeting is going to be arranged on the island."

"Are you telling me that the President will be coming to The Facility?" Kane asked.

"Not only the President, but the leaders of Russia, China, Great Britain, and France. It's going to be a conference on the members of the United Nations Security Council."

"How'd he arrange that?" Chief Bukowski exploded.

"That was part of his master plan all along. He's had over two hundred of his so-called 'guests' at The Facility. All countries were represented, and each person Mica selected was in a position to influence the head of his government, and make this meeting possible."

"I get it," Ganja said. "He'll get them all together and brainwash the whole bunch of them."

"What does he get out of it?" Jessica asked, looking puzzled.

"If he controls the five most powerful nations on earth, he then controls ninety-eight percent of the world's nuclear arsenal," Weaver explained.

"They could walk out of that meeting and announce to the world that Link Mica is now the premier of all nations. For the good of mankind, they have decided to make one man the overall leader," Kane reasoned. "Every other country would have to fall in line, or face annihilation."

They all let that sink in.

"We've got to do something to stop him, Ben," Jessica said.

"How?" Ganja asked her. "If we pop our heads up, we'll be arrested for Townsend's death."

"There's something else you should know, Miss Carlisle. Your uncle Reggie Thornton's death was caused by Mica's mind-bending. It seems to be happening to every one of the people Mica had as his guest in The Facility," Weaver explained. "Before long, they either kill themselves or go mad. We've accounted for twenty-six people so far who've died by their own hand."

Kane thought of Karen. How long did she have? He remembered her actions as they had passed in the jeep.

"There is a way," Ben said quietly. "We'll have to do it from the inside."

"But we can't get aboard the ship," Ganja said.

The Undersecretary of State can. I intercept the Undersecretary and take his place. Chief comes aboard as my assistant. Once we're on board, we knock out the transmitter. One grenade in the Communications Room should do it."

"I'm willing to give it a try," Chief Bukowski chimed in.

218

Weaver hadn't said anything. Kane looked over to the Director, who was staring at Mica's ships on the map.

"I'll need some kind of disguise. It'll have to be good to pass Mica," Kane said.

"It'll have to be very good," Weaver said. "The Undersecretary happens to be an attractive middle-aged woman named Barbara Collins."

"Damn!" Kane exclaimed.

"Wait," Jessica said, "isn't she the daughter of some millionaire oil man who sent her to school in London right after the war?"

"Yes. She entered politics after her first husband died in Korea. She's quite a woman," Weaver said.

"Well, with a bit of making over, I could take her place."

"No way, Jesse," Kane said. "It's too dangerous."

"I'm open to suggestions," she answered.

"With Miss Carlisle as Collins, your idea might work, Kane. I don't see any other option," Weaver said slowly.

"Chief and I go with her or it's no deal," Kane added.

"I can supply you with the Secretary's security arrangements. I can give you the codes. And, we'll have to paint Brand's chopper into an Air Force clone. It can be done, but we have to do it quickly!" Weaver said. "The meeting is scheduled to take place is six hours."

CHAPTER 21

The sun was beginning to go down behind the broad shoulder of Signal Hill. Mike Mulhaney checked his watch and cursed the Manassah Bus Line for the thousandth time as the driver came to a dead stop in order to whistle and exchange pleasantries with the native girls. The bus had taken him from the Red Hook ferry on the eastern tip of the island, past the College of the Virgin Islands, along the Waterfront Highway, and finally to Market Place.

He got off and walked the rest of the way, slowly climbing up the ninety-nine steps of Government

Hill. He hardly noticed the remains of the seven-teenth-century Fort Skytsborg and its impressive Bluebeard's Tower. The tower had been incorporated into a hotel, but it wasn't the hotel he was interested in. He made his way to Hotel 1829, where the Americans were staying.

There were three stretch limousines in front of the ornate old building. Each of the limos had a small American flag sticking up from the hood.

As soon as he entered the lobby, he was stopped by a man wearing sunglasses. He had on a gray sharkskin suit, with a blue tie. An American-flag pin was stuck in his lapel.

"Sir, are you a guest of this hotel?" the man asked.

"No."

"Then I'm going to have to ask you to remain outside for fifteen minutes. We'll be leaving the hotel and then you may proceed to your destination."

"My instructions are to deliver a message to the Number Two Fox in person."

The Secret Service man sized him up. "Who is this message from, sir?"

"The message is from the Grizzly."

The man nodded and fished out a walkie-talkie from his back pocket.

"Simmons, in the lobby," he said into the black transmitter.

There was a moment of static.

"Go, Simmons."

"We've got a messenger here from Grizzly with something for Fox Two. He requests an eyeball, QSO."

"Send him down," came the scratchy reply.

"Room 114, sir," the security man said, and then turned his attention back to the doorway.

Mike was glad he hadn't screwed it up. When Kane gave him all the code words, he had started to get confused. He hoped Weaver had them all right.

Another security man, practically identical to the first, stopped him at the door. He had the walkie-talkie in his hand and was presumably the man Simmons had cleared his entrance with.

"Howdy," he said, not smiling. "I can't let you in to Fox Two. Give me the message and I will be sure that it's delivered."

"Can't do that," Mike told him. "This is straight from Grizzly. It's got to be eyeball to eyeball."

The Secret Service man nodded. "I've got to run this over you, then." He picked up a portable metal detector.

"I'll save you the trouble," Mike said. He reached into his shoulder holster and pulled out his .38 detective special. "Open the door, cowboy," he ordered.

"Hey, what is this? How did you get the codes?"

"You don't worry about that. You just worry about getting the door open."

"I can't do that! I can't allow something to happen to the Secretary."

"Look son, I'm no killer. I don't want anybody to get hurt. I'm an American, just like you. All we're going to do is sit here for an hour and then I'm going to hand my gun over to you. But you've got to give me that hour or you'll force me to put a bullet into you. Don't be a hero for nothing. At least not for a sixty-minute hour."

The Secret Service man thought about it, then pulled the key from his pocket.

"Open it, and walk into the room."

Mike followed him in.

A man in a tuxedo was sitting on the couch. He was talking to a gray-haired woman, her hair pulled back severely, wearing a pink evening gown. They both turned when the door opened.

The man's eyes went down to the gun and then up to Mike Mulhaney. "Who are you?" he asked.

"Name's Mike Mulhaney, and I have a little story to tell you. Why don't we all sit down on the couch and make ourselves comfortable. You, cowboy with the walkie-talkie, I want you to give the boys out front a ring and tell them that Fox Two has got the runs and the trip to Mica's boat is going to be delayed for at least an hour.

"Don't try anything stupid. I know all the codes and the numbers. Remember what I said about being a hero."

Karen Aztec was shown to her private stateroom by one of Mica's hostesses aboard *The Loyalty*.

She had been glad when one of the Security people had knocked on her cottage door and invited her to the Administration Building. Major Frank was there and welcomed her warmly. He told her that Link was expecting some very important guests from Washington that evening and he wondered if she felt well enough to join them. The Major said he was invited, too, and that they would take a chopper from The Facility and arrive early.

When Karen had protested that she really didn't know if she was up to it, Major Frank had reached into a drawer and pulled out a gorgeous diamond and sapphire necklace.

"Link felt you might want to show this off. He said no one but you could do it justice. He told me he'd really like to see you wearing it this evening."

In the end, she had agreed to go, and she felt good about her decision. All the moping in the world wasn't going to bring Robert back. Link was such a sweetheart. As busy as he was, he still took the time to see how she was feeling. She still needed more time to sort out her feelings about taking over for Robert.

She also had to think more about Kane. It seemed that every time she tried to concentrate on Ben, her mind would get fuzzy and her head would hurt.

Yes, she was glad she accepted Link's offer. It would give her a chance to be with people and give her a change of scenery. She also had to thank Link for his generosity.

Brand's helicopter had been painted olive green to give it the look of an Air Force helicopter. Weaver's people had just put the finishing touches on the new serial numbers when it was time to lift off. The painter warned Brand not to let anyone lean on the chopper because the paint still wasn't dry in a couple of spots.

Jessica had been made to look older and her hair had been grayed. Kane didn't know if she looked like Barbara Collins, but she did resemble the picture of Collins that Weaver's makeup man had used.

Kane grew a false mustache and a double chin. His hair was cut and darkened. With the sunglasses and dark gray baggy suit, Kane looked every bit the part of a Secret Service man.

Chief Bukowski was given a tuxedo. He fidgeted with the collar and cursed the damn monkey suit. He was to be a State Department aide. And Henry Brand was dressed in an Air Force captain's uniform.

They flew low over the inky black ocean and approached Mica's *The Loyalty* hanging like a small mountain on the horizon below them.

"This is Mica 114 on patrol. Request identification of chopper heading toward Mica 1," the radio crackled.

Brand swallowed hard and read from the card Weaver had prepared for him. "This is Captain Maldonato on Air Force Apple-Baker-Two-Two-One-Four-Five-King-Larry-Oscar-Six-Zero-Four. Do you copy?"

"We copy. Proceed to destination, Captain Maldonato, and welcome to *The Loyalty*."

"Thank you. Out."

Brand gave Kane the thumbs-up sign and lowered the chopper aboard one of the two helicopter pads on the large ship.

"How are you doing, Madame Secretary?" Kane asked Jessica.

"Some butterflies, but that's to be expected. I just have to remember to soften my accent. I'll throw in a few "you all's.""

"Don't overdo it. Mica will do all the talking. All we'll need is a few minutes to blow the Communications Room and then we'll come fetch you."

When the door of the chopper opened, Kane and the rest of the crew were startled by the glare of a huge searchlight. The assembled crew on board Mica's yacht broke into a round of applause. Somewhere starboard, a band launched into a medley of showtunes from *Oklahoma*.

"She must be from Oklahoma," Kane whispered to Jessica.

Jessica smiled and waved as a red carpet was rolled out from the chopper.

Link Mica stepped forward and handed Jessica a bouquet of flowers as Kane tried to melt into the background.

"So pleased to have you on board, Madame Secretary."

"Please call me Barbara," Jessica said.

"Fine, my friends call me Link."

"Then Link it is. I would like you to meet Mr. Matthew Kirk of my office. Mr. Kirk will be helping to arrange the details of the President's visit. He's the liaison with the White House staff."

Mica shook hands with Chief Bukowski.

Kane was impressed with the way Jessica was handling herself.

"May I show you around *The Loyalty*?" Mica asked.

"Perhaps afterwards, if you don't mind. We have a long agenda this evening."

"All right. Why don't you and your security people follow me to my conference room."

The conference room in *The Loyalty* was a wood-paneled room with a view of the outside deck and the ocean behind it. Link seated Jessica and Bukowski at the square table. There was a pitcher of ice water in the center, and beautiful crystal goblets.

Kane waited for Jessica and Bukowski to be seated, and then stepped out of the room. So far so good. They were sure that Mica hadn't recognized them. In fact, Kane wondered if he had noticed them at all.

Kane figured the Communications Room to be one deck down and toward the bow. He wondered how many of Mica's people would be guarding the door. One way or another, he had to put it out of commission. He checked his watch. Another five minutes and he'd make their move downstairs.

He hoped that Jessica could fence with Mica long enough to give them time.

Major Frank was walking down the staircase heading in his direction. He walked right up to the conference room door and spoke to Kane.

"I'm Major Frank. I'm authorized to be inside. I'll be working with the President's people to make sure we have the tightest security," he said.

"Yes, Major, you may go in."

"Aren't you going to check me out?"

"No need to, Major," Kane said, changing his voice and hoping the mustache didn't fall off.

Frank seemed to shrug. It was as if he was saying to himself that these guys couldn't make it in *his* outfit. He opened the door and walked inside.

Kane got a glimpse of Jessica listening intently to Link Mica. Chief Bukowski was writing on a pad. Link Mica stood up and introduced Major Frank to them. The door closed.

That was close, Kane thought and headed down

the staircase to the deck below.

There was a long corridor with staterooms on both sides. At the end of that corridor, at an almost ninety-degree angle, would be the off-limits Communications Room.

Suddenly the door to one of the staterooms opened. He continued to walk forward as Karen Aztec stepped out of the room.

"Good evening," she said, sliding past him in the narrow corridor.

Kane felt her eyes on the back of his head. It seemed to him that she looked startled as he walked by.

"You're Ben Kane!" she shouted.

He turned and put his hand on Karen's mouth, stopping her from making any noise. She struggled against him, to no avail.

Seeing they were alone, Ben dragged her into the stateroom she had just left.

Ben closed the door. "I'm going to take my hand off your mouth," Ben told her, "but you have to promise me you won't scream. Do you promise?"

She shook her head yes.

He slowly released her.

"Murderer!" she hissed at Ben. "Lousy rotten murderer!"

"What are you talking about?"

"You killed Robert Townsend!"

"Karen, you have to believe me. I didn't kill Townsend. If anyone murdered Robert Townsend, it was Link Mica."

"You're a liar, Kane!"

"No, I'm not lying. I don't expect you to believe me because you and everyone else in The Facility have been brainwashed."

"What do you mean, brainwashed?" she asked him. "How could he do that?"

"Through the headphones everyone is supposed to use at night. Maybe Robert found out that they were being used to enslave people's minds, and he wouldn't stand for it."

"It's just white noise. That can't brainwash anyone. Just leave me alone! I have to go upstairs and meet Link's guest."

"Mica sends out signals from this ship that are played subliminally on top of the white noise. It makes people believe everything he says and makes them follow his orders when they leave the island. Eventually, they commit suicide or go crazy."

Karen cradled her head. She seemed to be in great pain. "I don't understand any of this. Link Mica wouldn't do that. He's good and kind."

"You've got to fight it, Karen. You've got to try to bring back your mental defenses," Kane said.

"How do I know you're not the one who's lying?"

"Come with us and I'll show you how Mica does it. You know something about computers; you'll see."

"I don't know what to believe anymore."

231

Kane lifted her up from the bed. He stared into her eyes and touched her tenderly on the chin.

"Trust me, Karen," he told her softly. Kane held Karen's shoulder and walked her out.

"It's deserted. Where's the crew and security, Karen?"

"There's a staff party in the main salon. Everyone was invited. Link, Barbara Collins, and I were supposed to drop in and greet them."

"Nice and cozy," said Kane. "Hmm, that's odd."

When he had turned the corner, he expected to see at least one armed guard standing in front of the Communications Room. Not only wasn't there an armed guard, there wasn't any Communications Room.

"What the— It was right here. I'm sure of it!" Kane insisted. "The transmitter is right on top of us."

"Well, there's nothing here but a solid wall," Karen said.

Kane walked over to the spot where the door had been. He ran his fingers over the solid steel wall.

"I feel . . . it feels like a seam. The machinery in here is self-contained and probably needs very little maintenance. When Coco breached his security, Mica probably had had the door sealed up. He couldn't seal it completely because machines do break down sometime, even if they're built by Link Mica."

"I want to go upstairs!" Karen told him.

"You will. But first I want to show you how your friend Link turns people's brains into mush."

Kane was tapping the wall alongside the door. "There's got to be a release mechanism somewhere nearby. . . .

"I found something," he said, lifting a small Mica insignia plate.

There was a keypad in the wall, with fifteen numbers. Kane looked at the keyboard and looked at the door, then punched in the numbers: thirteen, nine, three, one.

The metal door flew open.

"How did you know that?" Karen asked him, her mouth open.

"I'll tell you later. There's no time now. Come on, Karen."

He took her arm and walked into the room.

"What the hell is all this stuff?" she asked.

From floor to ceiling there were all sorts of computers, with blinking lights, whirring noises, and the clicking of a daisy wheel printer.

"This is Mica's little invention that fools around with people's brain waves. He transmits it by using that big dish he has pointing at the island."

"I just can't believe Link could do something like that," she said.

Kane opened his jacket and pulled out two plastic explosive charges with fifteen-minute timers. That would give them enough time to rush upstairs and pick up Jessica and Chief Bukowski.

"What are you doing?" Karen asked him.

"I'm going to blow this evil machine back to hell where it came from," Kane said solemnly.

"No, you can't!"

"Sorry, Karen."

"Ben, listen to me, please! I don't understand everything here, but I do know one thing: If what you say is true and these computers are doing something to people's brain waves, by blowing them up you're preventing the process from being reversed."

"Are you saying that these machines can't be duplicated?"

"Look at them yourself, Ben. They're all Mica's work. He must have built them himself out of specially made parts. It would take years to copy this, and the only one who could do it would be Link!"

Ben thought it over. He had thought that the brainwashing was an ongoing thing and that if the computers were destroyed, everyone would immediately have their own power of reasoning again. The problem with that was the people all over the world who couldn't possibly be reached by the transmitter, and yet were still following Mica's orders.

"You're saying these computers have been programming people, and in order to snap them out of it, they have to be deprogrammed?"

"Exactly! I can tell—"

Suddenly Karen shook her head like a fighter who had just been walloped on the chin. She seemed to physically change before their eyes. One moment she seemed back to her old self, the next, she had that zombielike glazed-eye look of Mica's people. She was fighting Mica's hold.

Kane pulled out his .357 and checked the safety.

"Maybe we should go upstairs and invite ourselves to Mr. Mica's party," he said.

CHAPTER 22

Link poured himself a glass of ice water and tried for the third time to steer the conversation around to the President's visit. Barbara Collins had wanted to know about the weather on the Virgin Islands, and the shopping on St. Thomas. For a lady who talked about a busy schedule, she seemed to him to have all the time in the world.

Her assistant Matthew Kirk wasn't much better. He appeared uncomfortable and ill at ease. Mica wondered if he resented the woman being his superior.

Link tried again.

"I think we should discuss the President's itinerary at The Facility. We can wrap that up now, and then we would be honored if you and Mr. Kirk would join us at a small reception of *The Loyalty*'s staff and crew in your honor."

"That would be lovely," Barbara Collins said.

"You know, I detect an accent. It's slight, but it's there," Mica told her.

"Really?"

Chief Bukowski tapped his fingers on the table nervously.

"I'm pretty good at spotting accents. Let's see, I think I know your secret."

"Do you?"

"I'd say that you might be from Oklahoma, but you spend a lot of time in England."

Jessica grinned. "How very clever of you."

Mica beamed. "The other world leaders will be arriving on Saturday, and I think the President might want to arrive simultaneously with the First Chairman of the Soviet Republic."

"Yes, of course."

"I know the White House people will be concerned about the President's safety, but they needn't have any fears on that part. I've taken the liberty of inviting the Mica head of Security, Major Frank, here to discuss what we'll be doing. Major."

Major Frank stood up and cleared his throat. "Thank you. As Link said, I am Major Frank, and I will be in charge of the security at The Facility when the President arrives. I think that I can promise that the President will be in complete safety during his time under our care. The Mica Security team will be at the President's disposal."

"We had a little incident here the other day that you might want to share with the Undersecretary," Link prodded.

"Yes, a highly trained commando group tried to infiltrate our island."

"This had nothing to do with the visit from the President," Link added hastily.

"Oh, no, nothing at all like that, just a political tempest in a teapot, so to speak. At any rate, my forces repelled the three invaders after we identified and isolated them. I feel it was a wonderful trial run and illustrated how completely prepared my people are."

"That's superb!" Jessica agreed.

"I'm sure the Major will be working directly with the Secret Service on this. Am I right, Mr. Kirk? Mr. Kirk?"

"Oh. Oh, yes. I was thinking about what, uh, Major Frank was saying. Fascinating, very fascinating."

"Perhaps you'd be good enough, Link, to describe The Facility for us," Jessica said, stalling for time.

"That's something I never get tired of talking about. I had hoped that the young lady who will be heading the psychological component of The Facility would be here by now. Major, perhaps you'd be good enough to ask someone to find out what's keeping her. She's a very conscientious young woman and it isn't like her to be late."

"Be happy to, Link," Major Frank said, stepping away from his chair.

"Oh, here she is now." Link smiled.

Karen Aztec walked into the room, followed by Kane.

"It's all right. She's part of this meeting," Major Frank said to Kane. "She's with us."

"No, she's with us," Kane said.

He stripped off his mustache, and showed them the magnum in his left hand.

"I thought you said you took care of Ben Kane!" Link snapped at Major Frank.

"I . . . I don't understand it."

Link turned to Jessica. "Then you're not from the State Department, either."

Jessica smiled sweetly. "That's right."

"I hope you all know that you won't get off this ship alive. I'm personally going to see to your deaths," Link said angrily. He glared at Major Frank.

"Where's all the talk about love and world harmony?" Kane wanted to know.

"Let's go, Ben," Jessica said, getting up from her chair.

"Change of plans, Jess. If we blow the transmitter, we might not be able to bring the victims back to normal. Karen says the computers are Link's own design. Too sophisticated to copy."

Karen seemed in a daze. She took a seat at the table and stared down.

"Look what you've done to this girl, Mica," Kane said, shaking his head.

"You did it. You put doubts in her mind and they're working against my correct thoughts."

"Shut up, Mica. We're going to look in your stateroom for any plans or records you might have that can shed some light on how the brain wave machine works."

"You won't find anything," Mica told him.

"I think we will. You see, Mr. Mica, I have never seen a more egotistical son-of-a-bitch than you. You'd have to record your great achievement so that posterity would be able to honor you."

"As a matter of fact, I did take copious notes. Here's what you're looking for." Mica reached into his tux jacket and pulled out a small pistol. Moving quickly, he put it to Jessica Carlisle's head. His other arm was around her neck, stopping her from moving.

"My advantage, Mr. Kane. Throw your guns down, all of you! Do it, Kane, or your lady friend is dead!"

"Great work, Link!" Major Frank said.

"If you throw down your gun, he's going to kill me and you anyway," Jessica said.

"Toss it behind you. Now!" Mica insisted.

Kane threw his gun behind him.

"Very good. I love that chivalrous streak in people like you, Kane. It's that kind of softness

241

that must be corrected for the world and humanity to survive. We have to make the hard decisions. We have to weed the world of the nonproducers."

"That's why you killed Robert Townsend, because he ceased to produce."

"Precisely!"

Jessica went limp for a moment in Mica's arms. He relaxed his grip for just one instant, and she brought his gun hand to her mouth and bit him on the back of the knuckles. The gun went spinning out of his hand and rolled along the table, stopping directly in front of Karen Aztec.

She looked at it for a second, and then picked it up. Everyone froze.

"Give me the gun, Karen," Mica told her.

"Don't do it, Karen!" Kane said.

"Don't move!" Karen warned, brandishing the gun. "Nobody move!"

Mica smiled. "That's it, Karen. Don't let them get their guns. Hand the pistol over to the Major. He'll take it from you. That's a good girl. Give the gun to Major Frank."

Frank rose in his chair and Karen took a shot again, this time over the Major's head.

"I said nobody!"

"Karen, you're being very foolish. You know Major Frank and I are your friends. We want the same thing you do—a world of peace and love, where each person can follow his own road to happiness without fear or want."

"Don't believe him, Karen!" Kane said. "He

wants to enslave people. He wants to make everyone over in his own image and take away people's identity. He doesn't care about human life. He just wants to play God!"

"For once, you're partially right, Kane. I don't care about individual human life. My goal is much more important. I want to preserve mankind on this planet. I can't allow emotions from stopping my work."

"You killed Robert Townsend," Karen said, turning to look at Mica as if seeing him for the first time.

"Yes, he was no longer needed. You were much more important to our work. I wanted you to head The Facility. He would have been a danger to what we believed in. He would have stopped us from reaching our goal."

"He was just a kind, gentle man."

Major Frank fell forward over the table, trying to make a grab for the gun. He pulled it out of Karen's hand and had it for a second. Kane dived head first on the top of the conference table and held Major Frank's hand down. He clipped Frank on the jaw with his left hand, and the Major fell back, releasing the gun.

Jessica rushed over to comfort Karen, who was weeping.

"Now, let's get back to those notes of yours," Kane said to Mica.

Mica slowly reached into his jacket and pulled out a thick notebook. He handed it to Kane reluctantly. Each page was filled with scrawled writing and diagrams. Mica described everything, from how he built the computers in order to send the altered brain wave patterns, to his master plan of subjugating the major governments of the world.

Kane could see immediately that Karen was right. If they had blown up the transmitter computers, the people who had gone through Mica's Facility would have been in deep trouble. There would have been no way to bring them back.

Ben noticed there was a chapter entitled "Reversing the Process." Those three pages had been ripped out.

"You're missing some pages, Mica."

"Oh, you noticed."

"Where are they?"

"In a place you'll never find them. Those pages are my insurance policy."

"No deals!" Kane told him.

"You're in no position to dictate anything, Kane. In a few days, I will be the ruler of the world."

"Really? How are you going to do that if you're dead?"

"What's that supposed to mean?" Mica asked him. "Is that a threat of some kind?"

"No threat, Mica, just a fact. If you don't give us those other pages, you're going to be killed."

"You couldn't kill me, Kane. It's not in your nature to kill an unarmed man."

"That's part of my weakness, isn't it, Link? Well, you're right. I can't kill you. But Chief here has no compunctions at all about it."

Chief stepped next to Kane. He took the small pistol from the table and aimed at Mica's head.

"I don't believe you."

"You're only one person, Link, and you control many deaths. I won't be able to help the people out there who have gone through your little brain-picker university, but I sure in hell can stop anybody else from having it happen to them—including the President and the other heads of state," Kane told him.

"I'm not afraid to die," Mica said, staring right into Chief's eyes.

"No, Link! You can't let them shoot you," the Major said frantically.

"They're bluffing," Mica said smugly.

"You can't point your gun at Link Mica. He's the savior of the world." Major Frank bellowed and ran at Chief.

Chief turned and pumped three bullets into Major Frank's chest. The Major's mouth opened wide, and he tumbled backward over the top of his chair.

"No bluff," Kane said quietly.

Something inside Link Mica seemed to crack. He looked down at the body of Major Frank and then back up to Chief, who aimed the gun right between his eyes. Mica reached out to take a sip of the ice water in front of him. His hand was shaking.

"I'll give you the three pages, on one condition.

I have to go free."

"No way!"

"Think about it, Kane. I'll be gone. My plan is ruined. The people who have been programmed can all be restored to the way they were. You owe it to Karen, don't you?"

Kane looked at Karen Aztec. She was little better than the people who were in Mica's cell blocks. The thought of those people enraged Kane again.

"Can everyone be restored? Even those people in the basement of the Security Building?"

"Yes. Anyone can use the process, once they know how to do it. Without my explanation, it'd be impossible to figure it out in three lifetimes."

"Chief, what do you think?" Kane asked Bukowski, who had been quiet up till now.

"His miserable life can't stack up against the rest, Ben. If there's a chance to save them, let's do it. We've got enough in that book of his to bury him."

Kane looked over at Karen, who was staring at the ceiling and crying silently.

"All right, Mica. You've got a deal."

"You'll have to take the chopper and go with me back to the island," Link said. "I've got the pages hidden in the Administration Building."

"This had better not be a trick," Kane told him.

"It's not. I'm taking a chance, too. How do I know that I can trust you?"

"Because you recognized that chivalrous weakness in us. We keep our agreements," Ben said sarcastically.

"What about him, Commander?" Chief asked. He pointed to Major Frank.

"Link will take care of that for us. He's going to call one of his Security people and tell them they have to leave the door locked and make sure no one comes in here. Those robots will guard this room for the next hundred years," Kane said.

Mica made the arrangements.

"Chief, you walk behind him. If he says one thing to anyone, or even looks funny, blast him!"

"That would be a pleasure," Chief replied.

They made their way to the top deck and the helicopter pad.

Henry Brand came out to greet them. "What's this?" he said when he saw Mica.

"Change of plans. Get in and ferry us over to Mica Island," Kane told him.

"Great!" Henry said kiddingly. "I've heard so much about the place, I was feeling left out by never having the chance to go there."

"Mr. Mica will get on the radio and explain to all his cutters and cruisers that we're going to show the Undersecretary of State the island Facility, and they should make no attempt to stop us. Isn't that right, Link?"

"Yes," Mica grumbled.

The chopper's rotors began to spin, and some of the crew of *The Loyalty* came on deck.

"Wave to them, Jessica," Ben told her. "You too,

Mica. Give them all a big wave."

He jabbed the magnum into Mica's ribs. The billionaire industrialist waved to the people below.

Henry got the chopper into the air, swooped starboard, and nosed it toward Mica Island.

CHAPTER 23

"It's an interesting story, Mr. Mulhaney, if that's your real name. But I'm not sure I believe it."

"I don't believe a word of it, Barbara," Matthew Kirk told his boss. "Link Mica is one of the most respected and philanthropic men that America has ever produced."

"Yes, he has an outstanding background," Collins agreed.

"What proof does this man have? We're supposed to sit here, while he holds a gun on us, and buy this cock-and-bull story?"

"I'm not asking you to buy it. When Ben Kane

told me the story I thought he had gone off the deep end, too. But I know Ben Kane, and I trust him. This fellow Mica is planning to control the world. It's as plain as that. I don't make a habit of detaining Undersecretaries of State. I've fought for my country, and I was decorated for my actions. I've got a hell of a lot to lose here and nothing to gain. In ten minutes you get the gun, and I go off to prison. The only thing I'm asking is that you check my story out."

"I wouldn't waste my time," Kirk said indignantly.

Barbara Collins stared at Mike Mulhaney. "Matthew, I have the feeling that this man is telling us the truth as he knows it."

"Barbara, you can't be serious!"

"I am serious, Matthew. I told you before we came here, this conference makes absolutely no sense. I couldn't understand why certain people were so intent on having it done. It won't hurt to make a few inquiries. Please hand me the phone."

"I think you're going to make a fool of yourself on this one," Matthew told her.

He reluctantly handed her the hotel phone.

"No, I'm not. I'll just blame everything on you," she said seriously.

"That's not funny, Barbara," Kirk said, sighing.

"I want to call Mr. Hilton Bradley, please, in Washington, D.C.," she told the operator. "Hilly heads a large private detective agency," she explained to Mike. "I'm going to ask him to find out about three of the President's advisors. I want to know if they've dropped out of sight any time over the last six months for ten-day intervals. They have been strange lately."

"Can this Hilton Bradley be trusted?" Mike asked her.

"About this, yes. About other things, I doubt it. He's my husband."

"I'm telling you, this is going to backfire in our faces," Matthew Kirk said.

Brand landed the chopper on the pad on top of the Administration Building.

"You want me to stay on board, Ben?" he asked.

"Yeah. This is our bus home, so keep an eye on her. Jesse, you stay here with Karen. We'll be back as soon as we get what we need."

"Okay, Ben," Jess nodded.

Karen was sitting in a fetal position on the floor, slowly rocking back and forth. Ben couldn't bear looking at her.

"Let's go, Mica." He pushed him a little harder than he should have, getting out of the chopper.

The three men walked down the short staircase to Mica's private office. There was an entrance directly from the stairs so they didn't have to see anyone. The office was practically bare. There was the large Mica banner, of course, a desk, couch, chair, and phone console.

Mica went behind his desk and opened a drawer. Chief pulled him away. He took a pistol out of the drawer.

"You don't give up, do you?" he asked him.

"I wasn't going for the pistol."

"Search the desk!" Kane ordered.

They went through every drawer and found nothing but some pencils, papers, and a calculator.

"He's playing with us, Ben," Chief said.

"I don't know what your game is, Mica, but you better come up with those pages—fast!" Ben said. "The three pages and a list of everybody who's either worked or been a guest in The Facility."

"That wasn't part of our deal," Mica snapped.

"Neither was this," Ben said, holding the pistol. "No more games, Mica."

"There's a small calculator over there. Give it to me," Mica said.

Bukowski looked over the calculator and showed it to Kane. Kane nodded and Chief handed it to Mica.

"This isn't a real calculator," Mica said. "It's a portable keypad."

Even as a prisoner, Kane noted, Mica couldn't help showing off.

"If you look closely, this calculator has numbers up to fifteen." He went to the wall behind the couch. "This looks like a plain wall, doesn't it, but when I press in the code . . ."

"Thirteen, nine, three, one," Kane said drily.

Mica whirled on him. "Who told you?"

"Nobody. What else would you use? Your name is stamped on everything that stands still for a second. Naturally, you'd use the numerical equivalent of your name in the alphabet for your code. Put them together, they spell egomaniac."

"It's easy to remember," Mica mumbled.

He pushed in the code, and where there was a blank wall, a seam opened up, revealing a secret room, eight feet deep and four feet wide. The walls were covered with shelves; technical books were on all of them. It looked like thousands.

"Quite a library," Kane said, looking in.

"Don't go in, Skip," Bukowski said. "It could be booby-trapped."

"You walk in first, Mica," Kane told him.

Mica laughed to himself and walked into the room. Kane followed. Link walked to a middle shelf on the far wall and pulled down a looseleaf book. He opened it and withdrew three pages. They looked exactly like the other pages Ben was carrying from the black notebook.

Ben looked at them quickly. They were the genuine article. He couldn't understand it, but it was labeled as "a technique to reverse the process of altering brain wave function."

"Okay, Kane?"

"Now the list," Kane told him.

Mica shrugged. "Why not? It won't do me any good now."

He reached up and pulled down another looseleaf notebook, near the opening of the small room.

"Here's what you're looking for," he told Ben.

Kane opened the looseleaf and looked at the pages. Each page had a name, a biography, a date of arrival and date of departure from The Facility, and a specific task assigned through the brain-washing technique.

Kane took his eyes off Mica just for a second to look at the material. That was all Link needed. Mica shoved Kane forward into Bukowski. When they recovered their balance, the steel seam on the wall had dropped down and closed Link in the room. He had the keypad with him.

"What the hell is he up to?" Chief asked.

"We can't get him out of there. The hell with it, we've got what we came for. Let's get out of here."

They were halfway up the stairs to the roof when they heard Mica's voice. The voice filled the stairwell and reverberated throughout the building and all over the island. Mica was able to tap into the loudspeaker system, his voice booming through the night air.

"ATTENTION, ALL PERSONNEL. THIS IS LINK MICA. ATTENTION. WE HAVE AN EMERGENCY ON THE ISLAND. THERE IS A HELICOPTER TAKING OFF FROM THE AD-MINISTRATION BUILDING. THIS CHOPPER MUST BE STOPPED. THIS CHOPPER MUST BE SHOT DOWN. I REPEAT. BRING DOWN THE U.S. AIR FORCE CHOPPER AT ALL COSTS."

Henry helped them into the helicopter. "Hurry up, Chief," he yelled. "The voice of God just ordered us to be a sacrifice."

With Chief on board, Henry slipped behind the controls. "Hang on, everybody. We're getting out of here."

He raised the bird and headed out to the ocean. Down below them, they could see people running along under them. Some were aiming rifles.

"Turn it around!" Kane ordered.

"Are you crazy, Ben!"

"Turn it around, and head for the Security Building. That's the one farthest back the other way."

"But if we make it out to the ocean . . ."

"Then we'll be shot down by the cutters," Kane said. "Damn it, Henry! Do what I tell you."

"Aye, aye, sir."

Henry twirled the stick and turned the chopper 180 degrees. He pointed its nose at the Security Building.

"Can't it go faster?" Kane asked him.

"We're on max. Don't forget, I usually get paid by the hour."

"Go behind the building. There should be a chopper pad back there. Yeah, over there." Ben pointed. "Set her down fast."

There were two other choppers on the landing pad.

"Dragonflies!" Henry shouted.

They touched ground. There were two Mica Security men running ahead of them toward the big war choppers.

"Those two are mine," Kane told him. "Henry and Chief, squire the girls to the chopper on the left."

They jumped out of the chopper. Out of the corner of his eye, Ben saw the two Mica people climbing into the cockpits of the Dragonflies.

Kane stood in a shooter's position. His legs were outstretched and he had both hands on his pistol. The gun coughed once, and Kane's arms recoiled with the force of the shot. The gun coughed again. Two dead Security people were lying on the ground.

"Put one of your packages over here," Kane told the Chief, pointing to the belly of Brand's chopper. "Give it a five-minute blow," Kane said.

"Oh, man!" Henry whined as he pulled the girls out of the chopper. "It isn't even paid for yet."

"Don't worry, I'll buy you a new one," Kane said.

He ran toward the other chopper. There were twin Dragonflies on the pad, and Kane put the other lethal package under the one on the right.

Bullets seemed to rain out from everywhere. Kane rolled over one of the two men on the ground. He patted his pockets and came up with the ignition keys. He tossed them to Henry, who was already inside with Chief and the two women. Kane climbed aboard, and Henry lifted the chopper about a foot in the air. It was crowded, with five on board; the chopper was built to carry only four. A group of seven Mica Security people were running toward them.

"Now take us over the ocean," Kane told Henry.

"Yessir! Man, does this baby have pep!"

"They're coming after us," Chief yelled.

Two orange fireballs exploded in the sky behind them, vaporizing the Security people who had tried to follow them.

"Home, James," Kane said.

He leaned back and lit one of his El Presidentes.

CHAPTER 24

Mike had told Lee Wong, the inn's chef, that he wanted to throw a shindig at the Rainbow that would be the event of the year. The master chef responded with a buffet table stocked with dishes of stuffed plantains, rice with beans and meat, *calabaza, cochon de lait*, lamb and *turtuga*. The dessert table was a brilliant Caribbean splash of colorful tropical fruits — pineapples, bananas, coconuts, guavas, mangoes, and all kinds of citrus fruits.

"How are we set up for rum?" Mike wanted to know.

"We got all kinds of drinks, Mr. Mike. We got daiquiri, piña colada, planter's punch, and the West Indian coffee from Hispaniola to help make them sober later."

"Let's have no talk of being sober tonight, Lee," Mike kidded, rubbing his palms together, his face flushed with happy anticipation.

Just twenty-four hours ago he had been taken by an extremely angry Secret Service agent to the jail on Charlotte Amalie. There, Walt Gordon, District Marshall of the U.S. Virgin Islands, took him into custody and assured the Secret Service men that he, Gordon, would take "good care" of Mulhaney. He gave the agent a wink, implying Mulhaney would be treated to a beating for his brash actions. When the agent and Matthew Kirk left, Walt walked over to Mike's cell and let him out.

"What the hell has gotten into you, you flea-bitten old fool? What'd you do, help yourself to a keg of the Rainbow's rotgut? Come on, you and me will sit this one out in my office. I can't have you in a cell. No self-respecting prisoner would want to be in a place once habited by Mike Mulhaney. It might just stop all the crime on the islands and I'll be out of a job," Gordon told him.

Gordon brought out a bottle of rum and a deck of cards, and the two men played canasta while Mike explained his story to Gordon.

"I'll tell you something, Mike," Gordon said, suddenly turning serious. "I myself got a memo from some brass hat in Washington instructing me to show Link Mica every courtesy in any dealings that I might have with him. I was further told that if it seemed any law might be broken by Mica, I was to leave it alone and send the information posthaste to this big shot and he'd take care of it personally. I've never seen anything like that," Gordon said, shaking his head.

"Well, that fits in with what Kane told me," Mulhaney agreed. He threw down two cards and wrote down his points.

"This Kirk fellow says they're going to investigate your charges."

"Um hmm."

"I hope Kane comes back from Mica Island with enough hard evidence to satisfy Kirk and Ms. Collins so they can spring you," Gordon said, laying down a meld. He added up his score. "If you stay here another hour or two, you'll win my whole damn pension," he complained.

The call had come to Gordon some five hours later. Matthew Kirk was not pressing charges. He explained to Gordon that a prominent Virgin Island businessman by the name of Weaver had some documents that would corroborate Mr. Mulhaney's story. In addition, Undersecretary Collins had ascertained some new facts that were leading her to call for an immediate investigation by a select fact-finding body.

In the interim, Mr. Mulhaney was free to go.

Mike had gotten back to Barracuda Reef in time to congratulate Ben and the boys for a job well done.

They had gone to Weaver, and the director of Ultratech had squared things away with Ms. Collins. There was time for one nightcap at the Rainbow Keg, and then everyone had gone off for some well-deserved shuteye—but not before Mike decided that they should celebrate the fall of Mica at a party a day later.

Ben Kane tied his own bowtie, disdaining the ready-made ones that you just snapped on. He wore a white dinner jacket with black mohair tuxedo pants.

He knew Jessica would be at tonight's party but his thoughts kept drifting back to Karen Aztec. Mica's brainwashing had left her confused and depressed. The change from the intelligent, vibrant psychologist to the bewildered suicidal young woman was almost too painful for Kane to bear.

He had handed Weaver the pages of Link Mica's notes on reversing the brain wave process, and made Weaver promise that the first person it should be used on would be Karen. Weaver had agreed, but how good was Weaver's word? Weaver could only be counted on when his interests happened to coincide with yours.

They had gone directly to Weaver's office from Mica Island, and Kane also gave Weaver the book with the names of all the guests. Weaver had thumbed through the guest list, and when he was sure that Barbara Collins hadn't been one of Mica's guinea pigs, he called her. He suggested that Ms. Collins get a special investigating team on Mica Island as quickly as possible.

Ben walked off the *Wu Li* and headed down the dock to the Rainbow. There was something nagging at him as he walked. It was a vague feeling, like walking out the door without a wallet.

He stopped for a moment and took in his surroundings. Nothing seemed out of place. The boats tied to the dock creaked against their moorings. There was the almost hypnotic splashing of the waves against the pilings. A bell clanged somewhere in the distance.

He was about to put down his subconscious warning to battle fatigue when he saw the man in the car. After a while, you got to know the automobiles of the people who drove down to their boats at the Reef. But, he had never seen the black Plymouth Fury before, or the dark man behind the wheel who got very interested in his newspaper when Ben looked up at him.

Kane bent down, pretending to tie his shoelace, while he thought about his next move.

He could be mistaken, and the fellow might be just a guest of one of the fishermen going out for a night catch. Or perhaps he was a tourist, coming down to the docks to watch the sunset and see the boats.

Ben walked down the path toward the road leading to the Rainbow Keg. If the man made an attempt to follow him, Ben had his 9mm MAB in his ankle holster.

Ben walked to a place in the road next to some tall brush. The man in the car made no move to follow. He ducked behind the weeds, out of the man's line of sight and surveyed the car once again. The man didn't move from his spot, and Ben was about to put his suspicions to rest when the man looked around and put down his newspaper. He got out of the Fury and looked around again, as if to make sure Ben was gone. Kane watched as the stranger stealthily walked down the dock to the *Wu Li*!

Now it was Kane who was the stalker. He moved slowly back toward his ship and the man who was boarding her, uninvited.

Kane reached the Fury and looked inside. There were no clues about the man or his mission in the car. For all Ben knew, he might have been a simple thief looking for an easy score.

But the beauty of the *Wu Li* was hidden, for the most part, below deck. Its topside exterior wasn't the kind of target that would attract a thief, not with the extravagant and ornate yachts on either side of her.

Kane could have gone below deck and confronted the man there, but it made more sense to surprise him in his own car. If he wasn't an ordinary thief, he was looking for something. And

Kane had a good idea of what it was.

It took the man less than ten seconds to open the lock of the *Wu Li*'s pilothouse. In another fifteen seconds, he disappeared below deck. Kane found an open door on the Fury and climbed into the back seat. He waited and watched. Ten minutes went by, and the man reappeared. His hands were empty—so much for the thief scenario—and he had an annoyed look on his face as he walked back toward his car.

He was a black man, approximately five ten, with very dark skin and a large flat nose. He was built squat, with powerful arms and a barrel chest, and he wore a cheap, rumpled brown suit.

When he got to the car he reached into his pocket and pulled out a walkie-talkie. He opened the front door without looking in the back, and slid behind the wheel. Kane saw him open the window and fully extend the walkie-talkie's antenna.

"Brock," he said into the oblong box.

There was the crackle of static and a voice answered, "Come in, Brock."

"I tossed the boat. It's not on board."

"You're sure?"

Brock paused a few seconds. "If I tell you it's not on board, that's the gospel."

"Okay, Brock, take it easy. Come on in," the voice on the talkie said.

Brock switched off the communicator and laid it down on the seat next to him.

"Are you sure?" he mumbled mockingly.

265

He had a voice that didn't go with the rest of him. It was a deep baritone, cultured and refined.

Kane waited until he put the key in the ignition before he stuck the MAB in the back of the black man's skull.

"Keep both of your hands on the steering wheel," Kane said.

The man slowly complied with Kane's order. A look of self-disgust crossed his face.

"What have you got to tell me about?" Kane said, patting him down for weapons. He took a detective special from a shoulder holster and put it on the back seat out of Brock's reach.

"I've got nothing to say to you, Kane."

"What were you looking for?"

"Screw you!"

Kane hit him hard with the butt end of the gun. Brock slumped forward on the wheel.

Kane reached down and fished out Brock's wallet. He thumbed through the junk until he came to the man's license. He was Harry Brock, and he lived on St. Thomas.

There were the usual array of business cards taken from people and then never looked at again. Then in another compartment of Brock's wallet he found what he was looking for. It was Brock's own business cards. They said: Harry Brock, Senior Consultant, Ultratech, Charlotte Amalie.

Weaver! thought Kane.

Harry Brock groaned and rubbed the spot on his head where Kane had conked him. Kane tossed his wallet on the front seat.

"You could have asked. I'd have given it to you," Brock said dully.

"No you wouldn't. You'd have tried to be a hero and I'd have had to blow your brains out instead of shaking them up a little. Tell Weaver he better not pull a stunt like this again," Ben warned.

"I don't know any Weaver," Brock told him with a straight face.

Kane pulled the six bullets out of Brock's .38 and handed the empty gun back to him.

"Get out of here, Brock, and don't come back!" Kane said.

"Don't worry, Kane. We'll meet again. I owe you one." Brock rubbed the back of his head with one hand.

Kane slammed the door and watched Brock put the Fury in gear and drive off.

CHAPTER 25

The party was in full swing when Ben opened the door of the Rainbow Keg Inn. He was greeted by Mike, who immediately stuck an Absolut vodka into his hands, and Jessica Carlisle, who gave him a combination plate of some of Lee Wong's gastronomical masterpieces.

Chief Bukowski, Gordon, Brand, Sir Phillip Carlisle, Ganja, and Miles made up the guest list of people Kane knew. There were two other men, and Ben counted seven other women of diverse ages who had been invited by Mike. ·

"Where did all the ladies come from, Mike?"

Kane asked him.

"Three of them are working girls, and two of them are rich divorcees. I defy you to tell me which is which," he said with a gleam in his eye. "The other two ladies are the wives of Jack Foreman and Chauncey O'Hara." He pointed to the two men talking to Lord Phillip. "They're settling down in the islands. They ran a car dealership in Pittsburgh and did very well. Now they want to live a little bit."

"I'll throw in a free charter for them if they're friends of yours," Kane told him.

"Thanks, Ben. It's appreciated. Did you hear the news from Ganja?"

"No, I just got here."

"Go talk to him about our friend Link Mica," Mulhaney told him. "Some of Ganja's people from the village who had been working on Mica Island have been deprogrammed, and he's had some conversations with them. It's interesting."

"They've been deprogrammed? Already?"

"The process only takes about three hours, I'm told."

Chief Bukowski hoisted a bottle of Absolut and freshened Ben's drink. He overheard what Mike was saying and filled in what he knew. "It seems Weaver took a chopper to *The Loyalty* and put his Ultratech geniuses to work on Mica's computers. Even with Mica's notes, they were having trouble until they got this fellow Hannon from the island to help. Hannon offered to help in the deprogramming in the hope he'd get some consideration if he had to go to trial."

"I'd throw the key away on that bastard," Ganja said, joining them.

"Tell Ben what your Island friends told you about Mica," Mulhaney suggested.

Ganja shrugged. "Not much to tell. No one has seen him. It's as if the man has disappeared. Everything is in a shambles. The Security force has no chain of command. It was Mica, and then Major Frank. With both of them out of the picture, the Security people are just sitting around in a daze. They're being taken, one by one, to the dorms where the Ultratech people use the same headphones to send the new signals to reverse Mica's brainwashing."

"Hey, Ganja! Take a look over at the door," Chief Bukowski called.

Sharon and Jacob Peters were looking around the room. When Sharon saw Ganja, she ran over to him and threw her arms around his neck and kissed him. Jacob stood off to the side, smiling.

"Thank you, Ganja. Thank you for bringing back my Jacob," she said tearfully.

Ganja shook Jacob's hand. "How are the headaches?"

"I don't have none now. I'm feeling very good, to tell you the truth. I'm sorry that I don't really remember anything."

"He just remembers up to the day when he was supposed to leave. Everything else is a blank,"

Sharon added.

"Well, except for the headaches. I don't think I'll ever forget those," he said, shaking his head.

"What happened to Karen Aztec?" Kane wanted to know.

Jacob shrugged. "Sorry, I didn't see her."

"We're getting married, Ganja," Sharon told him, bubbling with excitement. "We won't wait any longer."

"We'd like you to be there, Ganja," Jacob said, putting his hand on Ganja's shoulder. "You've been a good friend to Sharon and me, and I thank you, man."

"Well, now that we got Jacob back to the land of the living," Mike told them, "he's got to help himself to some of Lee Wong's incredible plantains. You too, Sharon. They say they make you fertile." He gave her a wink, and the young couple burst into embarrassed giggles. He walked them over to the buffet table.

One of the women Mike had pointed out to Kane, about forty with scarlet lips and a skirt two sizes too small for her, whispered something in Mike's ear.

"Now? Why, that's terrific!"

He walked to the center of the room and stood on a chair, then banged a spoon on a wine bottle to get everyone's attention.

"Hey, listen up, everyone. Maddy tells me that a big Lincoln is just this minute pulling up in front of the Rainbow. I have a strong feeling that the

Undersecretary of State of the United States is in that limo, so I'm warning yuh to behave yourself and watch your language! Somebody keep Che Che away from the piña coladas—two drinks and off comes her top."

Che Che, another one of Mike's entourage, joined in the good-natured laughter.

"That's a new twist," Gordon cracked. "Mike Mulhaney concerned that we'll embarrass him!"

"Quiet, everybody. Here she comes," Mike warned.

As if on cue, the door opened and Barbara Collins, accompanied by Matthew Kirk, walked into the Rainbow. There was a spontaneous round of applause. Ms. Collins seemed surprised, and delighted.

"Is that because I let him out of jail, or because we had the good sense to put him in there in the first place?"

The crowd roared with laughter, with Mike laughing the loudest.

"Somebody get up a plate for the Undersecretary and Mr. Kirk," Mike yelled.

"No, no, really. We didn't come here to crash your fun. I have some things I want to tell you, and then we must be getting back to the airport."

The people at the party moved closer to Barbara and formed a circle around her as she spoke.

"Let me say at the outset that we have no idea where Mr. Mica may be. If he surfaces, there are a lot of people who would like to question him about

273

his recent activities. Be that as it may, we've employed a local firm called Ultratech to work on the computers and transmitters on Mica's ship, *The Loyalty*. They have succeeded in supplying the computers with a new set of instructions which, in effect, erase or negate the previous instructions. I don't have to tell you how devastating that brain-washing technique proved to be.

"However, we are now having great success with those people on the island. They can be brought back to themselves in the space of three or four hours. It's quite remarkable, really."

"Has Karen Aztec been deprogrammed?" Kane interrupted her.

Matthew Kirk whispered something in her ear.

"You are Mr. Ben Kane."

"Yes, ma'am."

She gave him a broad smile. "I am happy to say that Ms. Aztec has been deprogrammed and is well. She has agreed to stay on the island and continue the deprogramming process. She has agreed to coordinate all our efforts on this behalf, and we're very grateful to her.

"Now, who are Ganja, Miles, and Chief?"

They stepped forward.

"And of course, our kidnapper, Mr. Mulhaney," she continued, walking over to Lord Phillip. "And I understand, Lord Phillip, that your daughter had a bit of a starring role in the drama aboard *The Loyalty*."

Jessica stepped forward and joined the men

standing in front of Barbara Collins. Barbara looked at Jessica with obvious approval.

"Well, I think the casting is just perfect. If they do my movie, darling, I'm asking that you play me."

Kirk whispered once again in her ear.

"Matthew tells me I've forgotten Mr. Brand, the helicopter pilot. Please step forward, sir."

She looked over the group and paused for dramatic effect. "I have been in contact with the President, and he asked me to convey appreciation for your efforts. He considers you all heros. We may never know how much your actions and valor preserved the freedom of our country and the world. He thanks you all—and so do I."

The rest of the crowd broke into sustained applause.

"The Department of State has asked the FBI to conduct an extensive investigation into all phases of the Mica empire. We've already landed twenty agents on Mica Island and another ten are aboard *The Loyalty*. In addition, there are various Congressmen and Senators who, through their own committees, will also be looking into this affair. I trust you all will be willing to tell them what you know when the time arises. Now, I fear it's time to leave, so once again, you have the thanks of a grateful government."

She and Kirk waved good-bye. After a warm handshake with Mike Mulhaney, they pulled away in the stretch limousine.

"That calls for another round. Come on, everyone," Mike shouted.

Ben Kane nursed his drink and walked over to Lord Phillip and Jessica, who were talking to the two American automobile dealers. Jessica saw him walking over out of the corner of her eye and broke away from the conversation. She took Ben's hand and steered him to one of the out-of-the-way tables.

"That Ms. Collins is quite a woman, isn't she?" she said.

"So are you."

"Why, thank you. Father asked me to invite you down for the weekend. Do you think you might want to come to Tortola, for some good chess?"

"That's one inducement. What else?"

"My father didn't mention anything else."

"I didn't think he would. The inducement I'm looking for has nothing to do with your father."

"I can't imagine what you're driving at," she said. "Can't you be more specific?"

"I want to be sure that a certain young lady's door will be open to a mysterious middle-of-the-night visitor."

"Then I'll tell Father to expect you," she said, flashing him a dazzling smile.

She joined her father and whispered something to him. He turned to Kane and waved.

Just then Mike Mulhaney walked over to Ben. "Ben, we've got a gate crasher." He stepped close to the ex-Navy man. "That snake Weaver is here.

He says he has to talk to you. He's upstairs in my office."

Kane nodded. He knew Weaver would try to get to him; it was just a matter of time.

Kane climbed the stairs to Mike's second-floor offices. It was here that he and Michelle tended to the shipyard and ran the Rainbow Keg. The office was filled with nautical momentos of Mike's career. There were pictures of Mike aboard the *Tom Paine*; Mike in command of a cruiser; Mike and Michelle fishing together.

Behind the large desk, sitting in Mike's chair, was Weaver. The director of Ultratech was dressed in a blue business suit with a canary yellow shirt and tie.

"Ben, we've got to talk," Weaver told him.

"I've already talked to Harry Brock."

"Brock? I don't think I know a Brock."

"He works for you, Weaver. He's a senior consultant."

Weaver made a face as if trying to remember. Finally, he just shrugged. "We've got so many people. They come and go."

"This one came onto the *Wu Li* and searched my boat tonight."

"Hey, look, buddy boy, let's not get sidetracked here. You have something of mine and I want it."

"How do you figure that?" Kane said, casually removing an El Presidente from its aluminum casing and lighting it.

"I organized this mission. I gave Ganja papers. I

supplied the codes. I—"

"So you did."

"I want the rest of the black book that Mica gave you."

"I don't know what you're talking about," Kane answered.

Weaver ran his fingers through his hair in what for Ben was now a familiar gesture.

"Let me remind you." Weaver smiled. "Mica gave you several bits of information. One was the list of all the guests at The Facility and the guests who had previously been there. Another was the mathematical equations needed to feed into the computers to deprogram the brainwashing technique. Link Mica made very detailed and extensive notes on his work. We had no problem with the deprogramming section. But when we looked for the original method he developed to initiate the brainwashing techniques in the same notebook he gave you, we found that those pages had been ripped out."

"No kidding!"

"I very rarely kid, Kane. I want those formulas!"

"You want to take over for Mica, is that it?"

"The ability to persuade individuals to steer a course beneficial to our country has an enormous appeal to my people."

"Would you also end war, hunger, waste, like Mica said he was going to?" Kane said sarcastically.

"Mica's ideas in themselves weren't all wrong, Ben."

"Sure, and there are still people who think Mussolini was great because the trains ran on time. The way you people see it, all you have to do is substitute your goals for Link Mica's and that makes everything okay."

"Listen, old pal, we can talk around this thing for years and not get anywhere. Why don't you save yourself a lot of grief and hand over the missing pages."

"I'd like to, but I don't have them. They must have fallen out when we ran to Henry's chopper."

"I find that highly unlikely," Weaver said.

"Sorry," Kane said, flicking his ashes in an abalone ashtray on the desk.

Weaver sat back in the chair. "I'm going to try and jog your memory into remembering where those pages might be. How does one million American bucks sound? Tax free, of course."

"Are you serious?"

"Very!"

"Get what you need from Mica."

"Mica's dead! We have it on good authority that he was aboard one of the helicopters that went after you."

"That makes me the only game in town."

Weaver nodded. "That's right."

"No sale. I don't have it. And if I did, I wouldn't give it to you."

"If we don't get it one way, we'll get it another,"

Weaver warned.

Ben stood up and started walking to the door.

"Kane, stand where you are!" Weaver ordered.

Kane turned, to see Weaver holding a gun on him. "Are you going to shoot me, Weaver? You won't get what you want that way," Kane said lazily.

"No, but it would make sure nobody else got hold of it. Now shut up and empty your pockets."

Kane smiled and produced his wallet, another aluminum-tubed cigar, a gold Dunhill lighter, some change, and his gun.

"That's it. You going to frisk me too?"

The anger on Weaver's face was replaced with a superficial smile. "Nothing personal, ol' buddy. Just doing my job. Hell, I suppose you wouldn't be carrying it around with you anyway. Think about my offer, and let me know if the pages show up, okay?"

"I've got your number," Kane said.

Nodding, Weaver put away his gun, rose, and walked out.

Kane retrieved his things, leaving only the empty cigar tube on the desk. He took it, stuck his finger inside, and pulled out three small notebook pages filled with the tight scrawl of the late Link Mica. He put them in the ash tray and lit them.

"So much for progress," he said as he watched them burn.

A dangerous gang of crack merchants threatens the Caribbean. Ben Kane and his fleet must destroy their operation before a full-scale drug war explodes in the next action-packed segment of series . . .

KANE'S WAR #4:
CRACKDOWN